When you're looking for a job, asking for a raise, pushing for a promotion—
YOU'RE SELLING YOU

When your career involves tangible items—clothing, real estate, art, machinery, equipment or supplies—
YOU'RE SELLING A PRODUCT

When you have an intangible product to move, yours or someone else's useful function—as an adviser, consultant, teacher or artisan—
YOU'RE SELLING SERVICES

When you want to encourage the use of an innate gift—as a writer, artist, actress, director or designer does—
YOU'RE SELLING YOUR TALENT

Learn how to connect with the real world, persuade people to choose you—your product, your service, your talent—and achieve the success in selling that being a woman has specially equipped you for. Read

THE WOMEN'S SELLING GAME

ABOUT THE AUTHOR

Carole Hyatt has an extensive entrepreneurial, teaching and social behavior background. She has co-founded, administered and been chief sales person for four corporations: The Peppermint Players; Childways, Inc.; Child Research Service, Inc.; and Hyatt/Esserman Research Associates. Ms. Hyatt works actively with clients in all sectors of domestic and international enterprise: with major corporations, government agencies, public interest foundations and the media.

As an educator, she has taught at every level from elementary school through graduate school. In 1975, she established The Women's Selling Game Workshop, which she conducts throughout the United States and abroad.

As an author, Ms. Hyatt has written *The Woman's Selling Game: How to Sell Yourself—And Anything Else,* and *Women and Work—Honest Answers to Real Questions,* Warner Paperbacks.

Her success can be measured in terms of over 8 million dollars worth of sales, and in the many thousands of women and men she has personally assisted in their careers.

She lives in New York City with her husband, award-winning documentary filmmaker Gordon Hyatt. Together they are parenting their ten-year-old daughter, Ariel.

THE WOMAN'S SELLING GAME

how to sell yourself... and anything else

Carole Hyatt

WARNER BOOKS

A Warner Communications Company

WARNER BOOKS EDITION

This Warner Books Edition is published by arrangement with M. Evans & Company, Inc., 216 East 49th Street, New York, N.Y. 10017.

Designed by Ronald F. Shey

Warner Books, Inc.
666 Fifth Avenue
New York, N.Y. 10103

A Warner Communications Company

Printed in the United States of America

First Printing: November, 1981

10 9 8 7 6 5 4 3 2

This book is for my mother, who gave me permission.

Acknowledgments

For her assistance in the preparation of this book, it is a pleasure to thank Patricia Linden. Her creativity, professionalism, and willingness far exceeded my every expectation.

Next I want to thank Julia Coopersmith, who acted as go-between, wet nurse, and staunch supporter at every time of the day and night.

I owe a special debt to Linda Gottlieb, whose original thought it was to translate the Woman's Selling Game Workshop into a book. Her enthusiasm and original outline validated this project.

I am particularly indebted to my friend and colleague, Judith Gerberg, who assisted in the original research for the Workshop by becoming an Avon Lady, giving a Tupperware party, and taking lessons at Arthur Murray and Berlitz, to name a few of her exceptional activities. Her vivid descriptions of her experiences and her common-sense application of them aided the shaping of the material.

To my daytime marriage partner, June Esserman, who allowed our office to be turned into a manuscript production factory during an active time of our business year, I owe much gratitude for her consistent understanding and support.

My special thanks to Barbara Toalson, Andrea Weissman, and Bill Harmon, whose talents and participation extended far beyond the typewriter and telephone.

I am grateful to Herb Katz and Linda Exman at M. Evans for their constructive editing and careful consideration of the material. Many thanks, too, to Diane Gedymin for her patience in producing the book's attractive jacket.

To Mortimer Levitt for reading the manuscript and offering his sage advice, a great thank you.

I am happy to thank my good friend Cloud Rich, whose superb sense of style and good taste has supported all my efforts for the past twenty years.

My appreciation to Burt Salzman for illuminating the examples of reality, communication, and affinity.

For my daughter Ariel, a huge hug and kiss for her patience in waiting for later to play.

For my husband Gordon, a very special salute for his agreement, participation, and extra-ordinary quality control.

Contents

Preface

This book belongs to you, and to the scores of women and men we interviewed who so generously share their thoughts and experiences with you. Their stories are the lifeblood of *The Selling Game*, the flesh and marrow of the anatomy of success.

Although their names and locales have been changed to spare any possible embarrassment, I wish to express my sincere personal thanks to "Alma," "Beth," "Doris," and all the rest who helped make this book a valuable guide for us all.

I am especially grateful to: Lois Clark, Selina Guber, Carolyn Setlow, Av Westin, Kathleen Westin, Suzanne Jeffers, Miya Gowdy, Belle Frank, Pat Cush, LaQuita Henry, Denise Cavanaugh, Diane Sharron, Jackie Reinach, Lisa Dubin, Elinor Bunin, Shelley Rappaport, Dorthea Elman, Lynda Wessel, Liz Van Patten, Peter Woronoff, Dina Dubois, Judy Price, Marian Maged, Judy Katz, Arthur Mayer, Albert Sanders, Margot Wellington, Barbara Lee, Joan Alevras, Enid Johnson, Joan Phillips, Tina Spiro, and Elaina Zuker.

THE WOMAN'S SELLING GAME

1

What Selling Is

The Success Factor

The essence of selling is simply this: finding out what somebody needs and providing it.

Read the axiom again. Clearly, selling is a woman's game. Because nearly every woman has been programmed from childhood to serve others, to please, to be the giver in a world of users and givers.

Since what selling is all about is thinking of what the other person needs rather than of your own desires and problems, the question is, why is your sales ability not automatically terrific? What has kept you from perfecting the business techniques men seem to have been born with, the techniques that are essential to success?

Statistics show that women now comprise 40 percent of the U.S. work force, yet only some 10 percent of those women hold top executive positions and of that 10 percent, a mere 6 percent is in middle management. Even more significant is the disparity between men's and women's earning power. In the professional and technical fields, women are being paid 25 percent less than men, and in sales they earn less than half what their male counterparts command. The time has come to repair these inequities by providing women with the selling skills that traditionally have been man's purview.

This book is designed to equip you with the tools and ammunition you need to give you that selling edge, to let you achieve measurably better results in everything you do. Having these power tools at your command will take the guesswork, fear, and mystery out of selling, and will enable you to succeed by giving you control of what you are doing.

> As a teacher I had gotten to be very competent in a very tiny compartment of the world. That was lovely for a while but when I wanted to break out of that compartment, I didn't know how to do it. I didn't see that what I could do in one compartment I could do in another. I didn't need to be stuck.

> Last year I raised $728,000 by writing grant proposals, organizing door-to-door canvassing teams and brilliantly conceived brochures. The foundation I work for is thrilled beyond belief. Yet I still haven't been able to get up enough gumption to ask for the raise that is certainly due me. When it comes to getting money for somebody else, I'm marvelous. When it's for me, I'm a total dud.

> I had some photographs I wanted to sell to a gallery and I called up and asked for an appointment to bring them in. She said, "Well, we have plenty of photos on hand and I'm not sure what the buying situation is. I don't think it's good to see you right now. Call back in a

couple of weeks and we'll talk about it then." I said, "OK, I'll call you back," but I never did, as a matter of fact. I translated what she said into the fact that what I had wasn't any good and she wouldn't want my photographs anyway and I might as well go on to something else. I translated it into avoiding confronting selling her something.

I've been in book and audio-visual publishing for about eighteen years and am toying around with the idea of striking out on my own. But I don't know how to present myself. How to get my points across. How to clinch a deal. How to talk on the telephone. How to even think of myself as a business entity.

I think I know why men have a greater understanding of the whole business process, advertising process, and selling process than women. We haven't been as exposed to the whole process: knowing when to say what and how to hold a person off without being rude, dealing with people.

I don't like selling. I'm not a natural salesperson. I don't have the knowledge or confidence to get up and do it.

The Brightest Ideas Are Useless Unless You Can Sell Them

If you are like most women, it's a pretty safe bet that you are missing the one business skill that will help you climb to the top of your field. Nobody ever told you how important it really is, and because you lack that information, you are being held back—nibbling at little slices when you could have the whole cheese. What's missing is the ability to sell—yourself, your product, your service, or your talent. Until you develop that skill, no matter how expert you are or become, you're in danger of being forever stalled in your road to success.

Whether you are an actress, designer, public relations pro, secretary, teacher, doctor of psychology, or volunteer worker, you are as certainly in the business of selling as if you were in a more obviously sales-oriented business: a real estate agent, a manufacturer's rep, stockbroker, boutique owner, or automobile dealer. The fact is inescapable, a verity. Face this reality: Before you can do whatever it is you do, you have to sell—yourself, your idea, your product, your service, or your talent. Somebody has to buy what it is you do or it may as well not exist. It's like the woman at a party who waits for someone to come ask her to dance. She is decorative, novel, and really quite interesting. So is an olive.

Selling and Status

For many years a woman's status rested on being married. Having *Mrs.* as one's title, a house to care for, and children to rear was what a woman's status was all about until about ten years ago. Then women began to seek careers. They soon found they wanted the same status and rewards from work that men had always wanted and obtained.

Unable to leave their housewife's mentality behind, many women sought safe career goals and careers. If they were going to work, they wanted genteel or women's work—teaching and nursing had for many years been the traditional standbys, and these fields were now expanded to include others—but not selling. Women tended to look disparagingly on selling, seeing it as a career choice that required the traits they most feared acquiring—pushiness and aggressiveness. Selling even today is still seen largely as a man's domain, something most women prefer not to become involved in.

Yet what most women fail to realize is that selling is what work is all about, and that if you look with disfavor on selling a product or service, you probably view all selling with disfavor. And selling is far more than hawking products or services. You cannot, for example, possibly get what you want from a career if you are not willing to sell yourself. Promotion, greater responsibilities, raises, new jobs, keeping a new boss or an old boss happy with your work, all involve selling. Selling is what business is all about, and the quicker women realize this, the sooner they will advance the way men do.

The Four Kinds of Careers and the One Thing That Makes Them: Selling

There are four clear-cut situations in which you're going to need complete command of selling skills. As you read on, you will learn how to handle each type as it arises.

1. You will be selling when the product is you. At some points and in various guises, you are probably going to be looking for a means to advance your career through a job, a raise, or a promotion. What you'll be doing then is convincing people that they need you, that it will be to their advantage to use and reward you for helping them succeed. You'll be asking for what you want, and the way you will get it will be through your ability to sell yourself.

2. You will be selling a product. When your career involves tangible items—clothing, real estate, art, machinery, equipment, or supplies of any nature—your mis-

sion will be to move the items from one place to another at a monetary profit. You will have to do this by convincing people that your product is superior to others, and that buying your product will be beneficial.

3. You will be selling a service. When you have an intangible product to move, yours or someone else's service, you will need to know how to persuade people that that particular service will improve their lives in some way. You may be an adviser, consultant, teacher or artisan, a service provider or an agent for somebody else. It's all the same. To get people to use the service, you will have to know how to sell it.

4. You will be selling a talent. If you are a writer, artist, actress, director, designer, or the like—a woman whose need is to express an innate gift—that expression will be complete only when you have given life to your talent by moving it out of the atelier and into the marketplace. Persuading people to buy your talent requires the same skills as persuading people to buy your product, your service, or yourself: the techniques and strategies of selling.

You still say you're not in the business of selling? That's what I said, too, when I got my first job in television. Having sailed into a CBS television station on a platform of little more than a headful of workable program ideas, I was convinced it was strictly my ability to churn out ideas that had sold the station manager on hiring me. Even after an incident that had me accompanying the sales crew on a client pitch to help explain one of my program ideas, I failed to catch on—still thought the client had bought solely because the idea was a good one. It wasn't until much later, when I was sitting on the other side of the table at CBS, buying other people's program concepts, that I realized what was really going on.

My revelation sprang from a week when four different people came in, each with an almost identical idea. That's not unusual in itself; you know how ideas often circle the atmosphere, ripe to be plucked. This one was good, and after hearing the same theme four times, I bought it from one of the four presenters. Then I began to think: "Something intriguing has taken place here." Since there was no substantial difference between any two of the four ideas, why did I choose one of them in particular? I mulled the question seriously, and when the answer finally registered, it was this. My purchase decision was based not solely on the idea, but on the person who'd sold it to me. It had been somebody who inspired confidence, who was able to communicate well and get me to agree, who persisted when I exhibited reluctance, who was willing to work with me and give me a chance to add my own ideas to the package. In short, someone who sold me. What became evident was that it's not enough just to have ideas—anybody can do that and there isn't a truly new one under the sun anyway. Clearly, if an idea is going to survive, you have to have the ability to sell it. And I became conscious of something about myself. My greatest strength wasn't in having ideas, it was in having the ability to sell the ideas. And I didn't have to be ashamed of it. Before, when I thought of "selling" I had thought of it as most women do: that it has dirty connotations of pushiness, deception, trickiness, aggression. I was mistaken.

Words Can Hold You Back

What selling really means is finding out what somebody wants and then helping him or her get it. It is convincing somebody that he/she wants what you can provide; getting him/her to buy what you have so that you both will benefit as a result. Selling is success, and success is when everybody wins.

Yet *selling* and *success* are words that can be abhorrent. They do not sit well. Their ill-repute goes back to the antediluvian convention most of us were brought up on: Girls that are nice are mere sugar and spice. It's a cotton-candy convention spun of air and little substance, and it loads the two words with some very nasty and unfeminine connotations. The implications of pushiness, trickiness, masculinity overwhelm and defeat us before we begin. They make successful selling seem unladylike at best and immoral at worst.

The response that makes a grown woman say, "Ugh, selling is pushy and dirty and it's not for me," comes straight out of the programmed reflexes inculcated in most of us during girlhood. We learned to play with dolls, paste movie stars into scrapbooks, stir fudge in the kitchen, and not make waves . . . while our brothers were on the baseball and football fields learning to sharpen their sales and bargaining abilities. Remember how you always got approval for being passive, undemanding, "nice"—and how the guys in the gang were rewarded every time they spoke up, made trades and deals, used somebody else's strength to help make themselves or the team look better? "Stay in the dollhouse and be still, little girl. Never mind what the big bad boys are up to."

Society's attitudes have begun to change. Nonetheless, many of us remain stuck with what we were brought up on, and it's no wonder we think *selling* and *succeeding* are guilt-edged synonyms for taking advantage of other people's weaknesses, being false, acting unethically. We never had a chance to latch onto the reality. But it's this: The only people—men or women—who act unethically are those who believe it is acceptable to lie, cheat, steal, deceive. If that is not your standard, you don't have to worry about the ethicalness of selling; immorality is not your style. If you are an ethical person at base and you are selling, by nature your concentration will be on ethical behavior: filling someone else's needs, providing real benefits, doing something nice by helping.

I think you'll agree that the time has come to clean up our mental vocabularies, destroy the stifling myths, and get rid of the negative, unrealistic notions that hold us back.

The Antisemantics of Sexist Mythology

He asserts.	She aggresses.
He is well-travelled.	She's been around.
He is under a lot of pressure.	She must be getting her period.
He's considering the idea.	She is indecisive.
He is highly organized.	She is obsessed with housekeeping.
He is powerful.	She is castrating.

Attitudes create labels, and vice versa. Somebody can call your new pink dress "chic" and you'll feel good about wearing it, or "frilly" and you'll doubt your choice. In the same way, people have developed attitudes and labels about women. Consider these stereotypes and the effects false labels impose. Knowing that the labels traditionally attached to women are merely societal myths can be the *Ah-ha* experience that unglues you from fear and activates the real abilities you've had all along.

Selling Is a Woman's Game

To sell successfully is to utilize the life skills you are already well versed in by transferring what you know from one environment to another. To put it another way: If you were to write your autobiography and translate what I call emotional words into career phraseology, you'd find that what you do every day is sell people—your husband, your lover, your parents, your children, anybody you think may need what you've got. And selling people is just another way of saying helping; it's a matter of changing the language in your head.

Manipulation: The Loaded Word That's OK

New language notwithstanding, here's a line that is usually a shocker: Selling is a process that is manipulative as hell, and you are undoubtedly one of the top manipulators of all time.

Does the word need laundering for you? Let's take it apart and examine what manipulation really is. According to Webster, the word means "to manage or utilize skillfully." In selling, that means shaping people's behavior through skillful negotiation, persuasion, control, influence, enlightenment, persistence. It's the same thing psychiatrists do—at fifty dollars a throw, thank you very much. They shape their patients' behavior and when their manipulative shrinkage works out well, we see it as a good thing. Likewise, when you shape your children's behavior, guide them to do what's beneficial for them, you're manipulating and you're doing a good thing. So why do we hear the word as evil? Why is it that what we do at home to shape behavior is benign and desirable, but the minute we make the same effort off home turf, we worry that it's aggressive and pushy rather than assertive and helpful? Performances at home and at somebody's office are not, it seems, equal. Not if you're clinging to yesterday's fairy tales, that is.

The Beautiful and the Damned

Fairy tales taught us some whacky things that we believed in when we were seven or eight years old. The stories always went the same way. There was the king, the queen, the princess, and the handsome young man. In the story, the king has a problem he cannot solve. The problem becomes so acute that he puts up his treasure, his kingdom, and his daughter as ransom. Whoever will take care of the problem can have all three. The lovely queen mother, of course, doesn't speak up but remains behind the throne where queens belong. In no time, a brave, handsome, clever young man comes along. He solves the problem, gets the treasure (the money), the kingdom (real estate), and the princess (the silent pawn). When the senior king and queen die, the young man and his bride take over the throne. He now wields the power and the new queen settles down behind the throne, like her mother before her, and is never heard of again. The moral: Good men are brave and powerful, good women are pretty and passive.

Once in a while the story changes and there's a stepmother in the picture. Staying behind the throne is not for this woman because she is wicked. She gets right out there and throws her weight around, wielding power right and left. Everybody hates her and in the end she winds up dead. So that's the second moral: Women who act for their own ends are terrible, period.

It's no wonder, with all those fairy tales drummed into our brains, we're afraid to go after what we want. We might get it!

The Fear of Success

Fear is the reason people avoid success—fear of what success will do to their lives, fear of not being able to succeed, fear of too much success, and just fear in general. The nice thing about fear, though, is that it's universal. Everyone has fears, and everyone has fears related to career achievement.

***Reality:** Success is scary, and so what?*

I'm a thirty-three-year-old dress designer with twelve years of experience. Four years ago I was going great guns, right at the edge of spectacular success. Just as I was about to sign my biggest contract, I mysteriously got sick and literally had to drop out of the scene. I'm just now putting myself back together, and looking back on those four years I can see now why I dropped out. I was afraid of the success that was coming. I was scared to go ahead because then I would have responsibilities. I would have to take care of people. I'd be in what I saw as a man's role and wouldn't be feminine anymore. No one would want to take care of me, ever. I would get into a money crunch—meeting overhead, making profits, that kind of thing. I wouldn't meet successful men because men don't want women who might be more successful than they. I'd be working all the time and have no room left for a lover or a family. It seemed as if I would have no choices left and would never be able to do anything else but work at being successful. I was afraid I was surrendering options, giving up choices. Now that I'm back in the market and starting my own business again, I realize that I don't have to give up anything to be successful. I can have it all—love, a family, everything I want. Success really can be a way of expanding my life—it doesn't mean shrinking back and giving up choices.

Get Your Fear Out of the Closet

Let's face this anxiety and get rid of one of the biggest, scariest barriers you can have: the fear you'll be rejected for looking pushy, and its consequence—that you fear success. It's what keeps many a woman hesitating at the edge, so scared she'll lose something she won't leap in and start winning. But look—even though being afraid to succeed is common among women and that puts you in good company, if you are afraid of success it's a sure bet you're not going to get it.

No fear I know of just vanishes. You have to tackle it as a reality. Acknowledge that it is there and get on with what it is you want to do. Take your fear along with you and work with it, not against it. Handle it the way you handle a car when you hit a slick spot. What you do is to go into the skid rather than try to fight what is happening. You act according to what is actually going on, collecting information, keeping your eyes wide open to the real possibilities of the situation, coping with the facts rather than conjuring up Cassandra's fantasies.

I'll give you a good example of how this works. You've been called upon to speak before a group for the first time in your life. You're scared to death and shaking like a leaf. Instead of standing there shaking, acknowledge that you're scared. Tell the audience, "This is the first time I've ever spoken before a large group and I'm so scared I'm shaking." There. The facts are out, nobody hates you and you no longer have to fight to conceal your fear from the audience.

It helps to know that you are not alone and I will tell you that everybody who is out there is scared at some point. Novices, pros, men, women—everybody is scared to one degree or another and the fear never goes away. But as the humanist Stewart Emery says, "The world is divided into two kinds of people: the people who are fearful and can't move ahead and the people who are fearful and take their fear with them." For a perfect example of Emery's second kind of person, look at Katharine Hepburn. She has said, "I am terrified of cameras." Having acknowledged her terror, she took it along with her and went on to perform magnificently.

Why You're Afraid in the First Place

Now let's take a look at your "skid," your fear of success, and work with it.

Studies in the psychology of women, particularly those thirty and over, conclude that our archetypical purpose and function is to be subordinate, to serve and to please others. The grand scenario calls for the males of the world to be the users, the females the givers. We are brought up to seek happiness in serving those to whom we are most attached emotionally—usually a man: father, husband, lover. By the same token, it is inherent in our social conditioning that men be the dominant actors; the implicitly superior race cast as leaders, rulers, managers, directors; the bold ones, the autocrats of the breakfast and conference tables. The successes.

Each race, the dominant (male) and the subservient (we, the female), has its own fears and prejudices as a result of this scenario. The Dominants don't want to give in to the Subordinates, and we Subservients are afraid of the Dominants because we think they must know something we don't. Since the whole business is a fantasy based on an *assumption* of director versus servant, the myth and its mysteries perpetuate themselves in endless cycle. The supportive little-woman image has been cast in bronze.

This, then, is the tradition many women come to maturity with: Socially and professionally we are programmed to think of ourselves as unequals. We are groomed to serve, support, depend, act for the good of others and not—perish the notion—for the good of ourselves.

Revolution on the Home Front

Came the decade of female emancipation and with it, difficulties, ambivalences, turmoil. The heretofore stereotypical girl-woman pursues a career. She is good at it, a winner. She succeeds by focusing on her own needs and desires. She is "selfish," "aggressive." She makes decisions, influences other people, gains recognition, becomes financially and socially independent. Suddenly the world is upended. All the old conditioning is turned around. The status quo is upset and, like it or not, so are she and her best beloved. Neither sees that all her experience in managing a household, rearing and guiding the children, reading and reacting to the signals men give out has translated directly into selling experience. They see her career success as something that changes the balance, alters the ground rules of her existing to serve him, not herself or others. It threatens them both. He fears losing the emotional, social, and financial dominance he is accustomed to owning. She fears that her success will rock their boat too hard and he will abandon her. That is a scary prospect, abandonment. Nobody tolerates it well. It's no wonder that women who do not understand what is happening today, who have not studied intimately how women's roles have changed, suffer from the fear of success.

You, me, all of us have been set up with every answer in the book as to why we should not succeed. Recognizing what the realities are all about is the factor that enables us to grow as individuals, and to succeed.

The Power and the Throne

If you are going to proceed onward and upward in your career, you want to feel comfortable about emerging from being the invisible supporter behind the throne. You have to be willing to sit on the throne yourself, to be in the seat of power. You have to take the risk, if that's what it is for you, of focusing on yourself, of controlling your own life for your own purposes, of letting go of all that programming that says self-fulfillment is a bad thing. It is the only way you will get from here to there.

Here is another useful translation for your career lexicon. Sitting on the throne where the power is does not imply that you are "ballsy." Remember the new language in your autobiography: Change *ballsy* to *titsy* and it means you are completely feminine. It means what you are doing is extending your experience as a woman in controlling and selling, in order to get what you want. That is the reality, and reality is the key to success in everything you do.

Also helpful to a woman is the network of collaboration and support that women are offering one another today. Where men often take a stoic stance and refuse to acknowledge their fears about work and competition, women are sharing these emotions quite openly. This book contains many statements from women who were willing to share their ideas, attitudes, fears, and knowledge with other women. It is, in book form, the kind of support system that helps us all grow.

2

Uncovering Your Hidden Agenda

A long time ago J. Pierpont Morgan made this perceptive observation: "A man generally has two reasons for doing a thing: one that sounds good, and the real one."

It's important to know the real reason you want to succeed, to be clear about what it is that motivates you most. Is your basic desire to gain money, approval, power, social contacts? Is there more than one moving force behind your wish for accomplishment? It's all right, whatever your answer, whatever it is you're looking for—as long as you are realistic about it. Often people tell themselves they're motivated by one thing—money, altruism, whatever they think sounds right—when they really are looking for something else. That something else is their hidden agenda, and a hidden agenda never really stays hidden. It will always emerge and take over.

You must be sure you are clear about the real reason

for what you are doing. If you're out there selling and are working on a hidden agenda, it's going to get in your way. In the long run, if you keep on kidding yourself with inaccurate terms, it will prevent you from judging your progress realistically. More immediately and concretely, you'll wind up collecting something other than what you claim you're after. If you tell yourself the desire for money is what impels you, when your real goal is to meet men, that masked agenda will interfere with results.

Recognizing your real motivation is not always easy; you may have to dig hard to discover it. I know, because the business of hidden agenda was troublesome to me when I first began my career. I wanted to be in the theater, and in order to do so I had to sell theatrical packages to people connected with summer tents, schools, civic auditoriums. At that point, I knew nothing about selling; I just knew that people had to buy my packages if I wanted to direct. So a lot of time and energy went into contacting people, using the techniques I'd learned in the dating process: get around, meet new men, charm them. Unconsciously, I was relying on personal appeal rather than on the benefits of the product I was offering. Without admitting it, I was really still looking for social contacts, and that's exactly what I got. I'd go into conference after conference, and come out with proposition after proposition—but never a contract. Despite what I told myself, social contacts were my primary motivation and business was number two on the agenda. The primary motivation won each time.

This went on for months, until I thought, "This is crazy. I'm supposed to be in there to sell a product because I want the money. I'm not getting the money because I'm just kidding myself about it. What I really want is dates and that's what I'm really getting. Since what I'm doing isn't working, I'd better start telling people what a good director and producer I am, instead."

Still not clear about why I was selling, I swung into an Oh-boy-look-at-me phase: "Here are all the wonderful things I've done. Please like my packages." I was looking for approval more than I was looking for business, and approval is what I got. There were tons of invitations to parties, choruses of what a great girl Carole is, how nice, how terrific. That didn't do much more for the bank balance than the propositions had; I hadn't figured out that what I had to do was learn what people needed and fit my product to their needs. I kept on collecting approval and no contracts, and it took a long time to finally force myself to reckon with the realities of what I was doing, so I could move on to concentrating on money as the prime motivator.

There's a surefire way of knowing if *you* are working on a hidden agenda: The universe will tell you so. If you keep on collecting something other than what you claim it is you're after, even though you sincerely believe your own claim, you can be sure it's because you're sending out messages that reflect the reality of your agenda.

There is no moral judgment to be made about real and hidden agendas. If dates rather than money are what you're really after, that's perfectly fine. The only problem comes when you deceive yourself with false claims. Recognizing genuine motivations will bring genuine results.

Stop Whining and Start Winning

Kidding yourself with smoke screens and blue sky gets you nowhere, and bores everybody else. The copywriter at the ad agency who keeps telling everybody *ad nauseam* how she's going to write the great American novel because "creativity is the most important thing in my life" is a pain. She's not only a pain, she's sidetracking her career by not honestly concentrating on getting more of what she really wants: money.

Margaret is dazzlingly pretty, fairly intelligent—and a total fraud. She doesn't know she's a fraud, but the rest of the accounting firm where she works sees right through her. She went to work as a junior secretary to the firm's president five years ago and, through tons of diligence, has worked her way up to being his executive secretary. Margaret is single, lives alone, and the office is her whole world. She waits on her boss like a slave. Nothing is too much. She brings his coffee in at ten on the dot, gets his shoes repaired and his suits pressed, works late nearly every night and frequently on weekends. Sure, he takes advantage of her apparent willingness, and she cooperates with a smile. But outside the executive office it's another story. Margaret does nothing but bitch bitch bitch to her co-workers. She's a maid. She's overworked. The hours she keeps and the tasks she performs are inhuman. Everyone's wise to her story except Margaret, whose primary need is, after all, being fulfilled. What she's after is the approval of her good-looking boss, her substitute for the love relationship she'd really like to have with him. By appearing to work very hard at being the perfect executive secretary, Margaret is able to conceal from herself what's really on her agenda. If only she'd stop bitching about it.

Why I Can't Do What I Really Don't Want to Do

How many women have you heard complain that circumstances are against them? They can't get out and do what they want to do because they're housebound, husband-bound, child-bound. In fact, they may not be bound by anything more than their own real, if hidden wishes.

Take Elaine. When she was in her twenties she had a very successful career as an illustrator for shoe manufacturers. She married at thirty-three and proceeded to have the children she'd always yearned for. During her first few years at home, when the children were little, the women's movement hit and all her friends went back to work. Elaine began to gripe. She wanted to get back into the job market. She meant it, or thought she did, so she ran an ad for a housekeeper and interviewed them by the dozens. None was suitable. She tried. She'd hire one for a week or two, but something was always wrong. One housekeeper didn't get along with the daughter, another couldn't hit it off with the son. One fed the children junk food, another watched TV all day. The parade went on and on, while Elaine kept griping about how much she wanted to get back to work. About a year after the parade began, the younger of the two children entered school and a miracle happened: The right housekeeper appeared. Or was she there all the time, hidden from an Elaine who really wanted to stay home with her children?

Too bad Elaine hadn't faced the reality of her objectives in the first place. Staying home with the children was perfectly fine, if that's what she wanted to do until they were old enough for her to go back to work. It's failing to acknowledge real goals, and falling for false ones, that causes dissatisfied griping.

Reality: *Other people can see your hidden agenda even if you've hidden it in a mental closet.* You *can take it out and see it any time.*

Get Your Story Straight

It's easy to fall for your own story, as Margaret and Elaine have shown us. Alibis and rationales for doing anything but getting on goal and staying there are a dime a dozen. You've spun stories yourself, admit it.

One good way to force yourself into acting on the realities is by role-playing. It's a technique we've used time and again in workshops and it works every time. What role-playing does is get you to voice and thereby to define what is really going on.

Dialogue will help you to clarify an issue, especially if you role-play together with a friend who's tuned in to what you are doing. Lacking a partner, try the technique all by yourself, switching from chair to chair if that helps you to get into the scene.

In this example of role-playing, there are two characters, the Positive Person and the Storyteller. You play the role of the Storyteller; if you have a hidden agenda, this is the role you play most of the time anyway. With your partner assuming the role of the Positive Person, here is how role-playing can help you get your story straight.

POSITIVE PERSON	STORYTELLER
I want to earn $10,000 more a year. To do that I have to complete my degree.	
	I can't complete the degree. My work keeps getting in the way. I have too big a work load now. I can't find time to get my house cleaned and finish my regular job. How can I find time to get the schoolwork done?
If I go back to school it will take me two years, taking two courses a semester, to complete my master's degree.	
	Besides, my apartment has to be painted and I need a new couch.
With my master's, I can apply for a specific job I've had my eye on within my own company. I need twenty more credits. Each credit is $300; $300 times twenty is $6,000. Therefore I need $6,000 plus two nights a week for the next two years.	

POSITIVE PERSON	STORYTELLER
	Six thousand dollars! But I need a new couch. I have to have the apartment painted. And besides, there is no way I can unload the extra responsibilites that already take up two nights a week.
I could let the house go another two years. The paint job would be $1,000. Instead of buying a couch for $1,200, I could slipcover for $200. I'd have $2,000 to start.	
	Well, that part's all right, but I simply won't have the time. And you know how impossible the boss is. He's new and I have to keep teaching him his job. It takes a lot of time.
I spend a lot of time complaining about my boss. Since he arrived six months ago, he's taken up at least an hour a day of talking time and at least another hour of thinking time. That's ten hours a week. The ten hours a week I	

POSITIVE PERSON	STORYTELLER
pend complaining about ny boss I could spend in chool.	
	I really like complaining about my boss. Every night over dinner, Harry and I chortle about his latest blunder.
will keep the pleasure of alking about him over dinner with Harry, but talking ver the phone to my riends has got to go.	
	OK, I'm convinced. I'll go back to school. I'll put it on my goal sheet as a two-year plan. But what about the rest of the money?
know I have money for his semester. I'll enroll immediately. After I've enrolled I'll start applying for grants and scholarships. If they don't come through, I'll apply for a loan.	

This role-play, as with all role-plays done honestly, ended with the decision that was best—in this case, to return to school. Or, it might have ended with the decision that the effort required to get a degree was not worth the pursuit.

If you cannot role-play, there are other ways to uncover your hidden agenda. As you do the exercises in Chapter 3, look carefully at your secondary choices; they may be indicative of your hidden agenda. Keep a diary or journal, taking special care to record your thoughts about your goals, and see if a hidden agenda emerges when you reread the journal. Career counseling is another excellent way to unmask a hidden agenda.

Ask your friends what they see as your hidden agenda. Really listen to the answers without defending yourself. We see our friends clearly and can identify their agendas with great accuracy. When it comes to turning the mirror on ourselves we go blank.

Remember, there is nothing wrong with having a hidden agenda except when you fail to recognize its presence and unknowingly let it hold you back from what you could be getting.

The best way to handle a hidden agenda is to unmask it, so you can deal from a reality base.

Reality: *Unless you are clear and honest about what you want, you are always going to feel gypped.*

to feel gypped. Those women who have discovered the value of having their own goals, as men have always done, are the ones who are getting what they want from life. The other women—the ones who want something from life but aren't sure what—fail to understand the process of goal-setting and, sadly, often fail to understand what it is that they have failed to do properly, why *they* aren't getting what they want.

Let me illustrate what I mean the way we illustrate it in workshop sessions. We use a crazy exercise there called "Puss in the Corner," a child's game, really. It's played with five people at a time. We mark off a square and have one person stand in the middle and each of the other four in a corner. The workshop leader calls out, "Puss in the Corner, one, two, three!" and everybody has to change places. That's the only rule: They have to change places. We go through this insane exercise five times and then we ask, "Who feels she has won?" Session after session, the answers are the same. Half the people feel they've won, and the other half is flabbergasted that anybody would believe they've won anything in such a ludicrous game.

What happened with the "winners" is that they gave themselves specific goals. "I wanted to be in the middle and I got there," they tell us. Or "I wanted to try each space and I did." "I wanted to have a good time and I did." At this point the analogy becomes very clear to everybody. In life as in Puss in the Corner, when you make up your mind to get to someplace specific and succeed, you have won what you are after. When you have no plan, don't know what's going on and don't care, even if you luck out by reaching a "corner" you haven't the satisfaction of having won anything.

Now That You're a Grown-up, What Do You Want to Be?

> I knew when I was nine years old and helped put out the school newspaper that I had to be a writer. Everything I have done from that moment on has been for the purpose of becoming the best writer there is.

It is a wonderfully satisfying feeling to have a goal and achieve it. But not everybody is born knowing what it is he or she wants to go after. The woman who knew at age nine that she must become a writer is fortunate, as are all those who are blessed and driven by a creative talent. They have a ready-made affinity for something and can at least start with a broad direction. For many of us, with no particular affinity or immediately recognizable motivation, the basic question of how and where to even start presents a quandary. You may feel that you want to be doing *something*, but have no idea what it is that will fire the vital spark of enthusiasm that leads to success.

Some people who claim they have no talent have solved their quandary nonetheless, by thinking through what it is they already do well and with pleasure in their personal lives, then transferring that ability to business. One of the biggest social climbers I ever met at college went on to become a society columnist. A great matchmaker with a penchant for putting people together at parties uses her catalytic ability to match up business partners, for a fee. A terrifically organized homemaker has made a successful business of organizing other people's closets. Every one of these women began her career relatively late in life and with no previous business experience, wisely basing her ideas and goals on a transference of what she'd been doing as a matter of instinct.

You Probably Won't Do This and You're Crazy if You Don't

Here is an exercise that can help you to see what direction attracts you most. There'll be other exercises in this chapter that involve writing things down on paper, too. You probably will skip the writing part and generalize in your head instead. The best advice I can give you about really writing things down is—force yourself. The act of setting things down in words will get you away from the vagueness we all tend to indulge in, and into being clear and specific about yourself.

This exercise is called "Paper in the Box." Each day for a month, write down on a piece of paper what it is you want to do that day. Don't stop to think about it. Anything that comes into your head is the right answer. Be outrageous, be practical—anything is OK. "Today I want to be a neurosurgeon." "Today I want to be an astronaut." "Today I want to be a nurse, a banker, a biologist, statistician, chimney sweep, blacksmith . . ." Put each of your thirty pieces of paper into a box and at the end of the month, take them out and tally them. What you'll see is a pattern emerging. You'll see that a significant number of your papers in the box have something in common: You have an affinity for doing things with your hands, you lean toward science, you like helping people, you have a penchant for managerial or statistical work. A direction will keep cropping up on those pieces of paper—something that you can start to explore.

More Ways to Know What You Like

There are a number of ways, in addition to Paper in the Box, by which you can discover your affinity. They're all useful and they're all valid.

Get Professional Help

You can do as Karen did, and seek the advice of a guidance counselor. Here is how Karen describes what took place for her.

> I'd been in the job market in a variety of capacities for twelve years. My last job, before I met and married Len, was as a buyer for a department store. I retired when I married, and for the past eight years I've played homemaker and hostess par excellence. I've worked very hard at creating a beautiful home. I give perfect dinner parties. My husband and I travel extensively and have many friends. But for the past two years, I've been restless. There must be something else more meaningful for me in life. I figured, I'll get back into the job market and get myself a $35,000-a-year position. After all, I worked for twelve years, I've done volunteer work for eight years, and I have a superb contact base. I've got to be paid more than a kid just starting out. Well, I didn't know what I was going to do to get that $35,000. So I went to a career counselor for advice. I never saw so many tests. And we had a lot of pretty intensive discussions. Finally, we came up with a diagnosis that felt right for me. As I said, I'm a good hostess and manager, and I have a strong interest in helping people through volunteer work. Putting those together, we came up with the idea of a career in hospital administration. I used some of those excellent contacts I mentioned and, through them, sat down with a number of administrators to find out exactly what that job entails and whether I would need any additional

> graduate work to qualify. Now I have a clear path before me, and I am so grateful to that guidance person. I mean, really, it was crazy of me to think I want somebody to pay me $35,000 right away just because I'm going back to work.

Besides availing yourself of guidance counseling, you can devote several hours a week to writing out lists of career goals and directions or what you would have done if you'd had the opportunity. You can read books and talk to others about career opportunities. Work at it, and a direction is sure to emerge.

Take the Motivation Test

Here's a third way to help you learn what turns you on so that you can see which direction to take. It's a way to uncover your basic motivation and ascertain what it is you need in life to win satisfaction. Again, it's a written exercise that will help you think things through to specificity.

Read through the checklist that follows and write down the word or phrase that you believe is your major drive, the reward you want most. Be very introspective and very honest. Write down the answer on a piece of paper and save it, to refer to later as your needs and self-knowledge strengthen or change.

Motivation Checklist: What's Most Important to You?

1. Money
2. Approval of others
3. Power
4. Status
5. Social contacts
6. Creativity
7. Challenge
8. Résumé and credential building
9. Other drive

It doesn't matter what your answer is; there is no right or wrong, no good or bad. Any of the motivations is valid as long as you are completely honest with yourself. And know this: The definite desire, the motivation you have written down on a piece of paper, is your strength. There is power in it. It is the fuel for your motor, the force that will drive you to your goal.

It's Your Life; Lead It

As women, many of us are so used to having goals set for us—by parents, professors, spouses, people other than ourselves—that we aim to please them, not ourselves. We work on being conduits for fulfilling *their* needs and operate according to *their* standards for us, and we believe that it's wrong to do otherwise. Self-determination is a mind-set we've been taught to feel is wanton; it makes us uneasy. We think that by focusing on filling our own cups of desire we'll deprive another person of our energies, hurt them by our "selfishness." And so of course we'll lose them. We'll be ousted because we haven't behaved according to mythical Hoyle. If we decide to grow and develop in a direction that's rewarding strictly for ourselves, goes the belief conditioned by generations of female subservience, we will wind up pariahs.

So what do we need? Something for us or something for them? It's easy to see why we're readily confused. It's hard enough for anybody, man or woman, to concentrate on self-development; it's even harder for most women because we've been so thoroughly catechized to bolster the needs of other people: husband, lover, children, those the world has long held are the Important Ones. They're our omniscient, dominant Wizards of Oz and we feel we're in conflict with them when we don't adopt *their* goals, identify solely with *their* needs, act as compliant wife, sacrificing mother, dutiful daughter. But remember what happened to the Wizard when the mythology was stripped away? He became what he'd been all along: real as truth and just like everyone else.

Again it may seem like stating the obvious, but the truth is this: It's perfectly all right to determine your own future and concentrate on doing what benefits you you you. It doesn't diminish what you do simultaneously to help your husband, children, parents. The affection and relationships you've always had will remain while you grow and develop in your own way. Setting personal goals and standards doesn't mean loss; it's a winning process all the way.

Tune in to Yourself

Women are so thoroughly unused to setting goals for themselves that in many instances they need to be taught how to do this all-important task.

> I tried so hard to be a good student. I felt so dumb and defeated when I failed my high school equivalency test. I just couldn't study right and become what my mother wanted for me. In order to make a living, I was baby-sitting. My employer kept complimenting my talented hands. I can cook, hairdress, and sew very easily. I finally decided to drop my mother's wishes and follow my own. I'm so happy and grateful to be doing what I want. I'm apprenticing as a dress designer now. I'm happy all the time, and my mother seems happy for me, too.

And listen to Alma, who's twenty-eight years old, has already had three successful careers, and intends to have many more.

People told me I had to have an M.B.A. to get into the electronics company where I wanted my first job. I took their word for it. I didn't have that credential and I felt so defensive and anxious about it that I screwed up the interview. Now I've learned to find things out for myself by asking questions, not to take what other people say as gospel. Or just blindly do what's supposed to be "right." I went for a long time worrying about that degree, and when I found a job at another electronics company that I liked, I went to school nights to earn it. Meantime, I got married and my parents said, "Well, you'll just have to leave school and your job and move to St. Louis with your husband." I liked my work, I wanted that degree and I liked Chicago. I'd traveled a lot when I was in high school and college, so it wasn't that I was afraid to go to a new city. I just didn't want to go. I chose to be in Chicago. I talked to my husband and we worked out a weekend arrangement that we both agreed would be fine. And it is. I've done what I needed to do for myself, he's doing what he needs, we have the time together we both need and my parents and all the other people who said I shouldn't live my life so selfishly, well . . . . It's been the same for me with jobs. My father always told me I shouldn't jump around. I should assess whether or not the job I was taking was perfect, and then I should stay there. That's just not right for me and I know it. I had really good experiences at the electronics company where I got my first job, and then I moved on to a biomedical company where there was more opportunity. Right now I'm heading up a university research department. I've decided, no matter what "they" tell me, I'll always be looking for a job if it means more responsibility or more opportunity.

Alma's career points up several success factors that are particularly important to observe if you are in the exploratory phase:

1. She has set goals that will satisfy her, not somebody else, and has "won" each time she reached one.

2. She has realized that it is not necessary to strive only for the perfect prepackaged life goal or job. That's an impossible fantasy and people who don't see the reality almost always wind up stymied by their own rigidity. They remain dilettantes, touching on this, shying away from that, stifled by fears and mythology.

3. She has built up the knowledge and credentials that have moved her on within her field of interest and that may move her on into others.

4. She has not been afraid to set goals and make commitments to them. She has learned that they needn't be forever.

The Only Sure Thing about the Future Is That Nothing Is for Sure

The thing that makes goals so interesting is that you can always change them. If you're willing to be flexible and open in your thinking—a requisite in every part of the selling process—if you're willing to experiment, take risks and detours, you will grow and change even as your goals do. Change *means* growth; in their absence is stagnation.

As a matter of fact, if you think back over your life, you'll see that you are already well attuned to change and its connection with growth. It is intrinsic in every woman's *curriculum vitae,* the constant in our lives. As a caretaker you have responded to each stage of your child's or husband's growth; you had to. What you learned when your child was a toddler or your husband a career neophyte simply did not apply as they progressed. You had to change with them, to meet their altering needs. Even if your role has not been that of caretaker, you learned to change psychologically as you grew from girl to woman, as male/female relationships around you changed, as the socioeconomic climate shifted. You're an old pro! How well you succeed in applying the concept of mobility to your goals depends on how keenly you hone your innate initiative and creativity, the qualities to convert from your past.

It's All Right to Change Direction

The process of finding direction and setting career goals entails continual change along with your own shifting needs, desires, ideas, and opportunities. It helps to know that goals are not a forever thing, and committing yourself to achieve something within a specific time frame is not an automatic life sentence. It also helps to know that experimenting to find the direction that's right for you is a course that's been followed by the most successful people in the world. Think of Christopher Columbus.

The Experimental Direction Finder

Let me illustrate by changing Christopher Columbus into present-day you. Say you decide, as captain of your ship, that you want to sail to Hawaii. You know the direction and you chart your course for the Pacific. En route you come across someplace else that's terrifically attractive. You stop off, are enchanted by what you find and never do get to Hawaii. File it. It's all right because you had a direction that got you moving in the first place, and it took you someplace you found you definitely wanted to be. You haven't drifted at all because you started out with direction; the detour you took was a beneficial option.

To expand on the options, Hawaii could have turned out to be where you would spend the rest of your life. Or you could have been going to Hawaii because you love palm trees, but you learned there's more gorgeous foliage in Florida, so you head for where the good palms grow. Or you may have discovered that you really loathe palm trees and can't stand hot weather either, so you choose Alaska as your new destination. What has happened is that you have committed yourself to a specific plan for a short period of time and explored it enough to find out that it is or is not for you—or that some opportunity along the way is far more interesting.

Flexibility combined with specific goals has given you the means to cash in on opportunity.

Chart Your Course

You, the explorer, have found a direction by discovering your affinities. You've defined your basic motivation. You've taken some experimental career trips—either literally or by mentally visualizing yourself very concretely in the role you want to play. Now it's strategy time. How exactly are you going to reach your destination? How will you get from here to there, five years from now? Certainly not in one giant leap. The way to get from here to there is by setting short-term, interim goals: productive objectives you can realistically attain without fear of committing yourself to eternity.

Again, getting your objectives down on paper where you can see them is one of the first and most helpful steps to take. On page 42 there is a Goal Sheet for you to fill in. You'll notice that it is blocked off in three-month, six-month, one-, two-, and five-year columns. Before you start writing things down, study the Goal Sheet on page 43. It's the one I filled in years ago, when I first decided to develop the Selling Game Workshop. Let me take you through some of the steps, to help in specifying what it is you should write down as your short- and long-term goals.

I started by figuring how much time I'd need for research, what kind of research would be needed, what the sources were. Certain parts would take three months, another stage would require six months; at the end of four years the research should be completed. I outlined each necessary element in the same way, noting the interim stages and time limits on paper. I listed courses to take, interviews to conduct, outlines to develop, materials to use, and so on.

I'm onto another Goal Sheet by now, of course, but I kept that first one in the top drawer of my desk for years, where I could refer to it constantly, reassessing and making changes every three months in the same way any corporation does. It's been a trusty friend as well as my conscience.

Goal Sheets are tools the busiest and most successful people I know use all the time. Allie, a dynamo who always has at least three different sets of plans going at the same time, underscores something else about writing down specifics. She says, "Unless I set goals, I won't know whether I've achieved or have gone where I wanted to go. When I'm depressed or angry or discouraged, I'll say, 'Oh, I'm not getting anywhere' and bury myself under that. But if I take a look at my schedule, my three-month or five-year plan, I can see that I've done everything I need to do and that this is what's ahead of me. I can see if my career is moving along at the pace it needs to move along, or if I'd better hurry up, or if I had better revise my goal sheet. Right now I'm on four roads: writing literry criticism, running workshops, getting into counseling, nd meeting some people in the book world. So unless I ave a clear plan and a structure written down, I'm apt to eel overwhelmed and get very entangled, or feel I'll ever get it all done and do nothing. But with structure, ll I have to do is tackle the plan piece by piece and it eems to just flow along."

Getting Down to Cases: How Realistic Is Your Goal?

n order to succeed you have to know what it is you want o succeed in and then you have to get down to cases. The world is a vast toybox brimming with alluring things o sample. And there's an even vaster number of people esides yourself with their hands in the same toybox, grabbing for the same things you want. You need to do ome homework before you leap into the fray, so you'll know which end of the box it is feasible to dip into.

One way we help people do this in our workshop is by using the Puss in the Corner exercise with a second rule added. We say, "It's better to be in a corner than in the middle and you may do anything that is necessary to get into a corner." The five players scramble through the exercise five times, and then we ask those who feel they've won, "How did you win?" The answers fly at us: "I won because I noticed everybody else was going clockwise so I went counterclockwise." "I hooked up with a partner and we strategized that if one of us gives up her position, the other could win." "I won because I got a corner four times." "I won when I got a corner once."

At this point we explain again the analogies of reaching game and career goals. First, the people who feel they've won when they've reached a corner, or goal, one

GOALS

3 MONTHS	6 MONTHS	1 YEAR	2 YEARS	5 YEARS

GOALS
FOR WOMAN'S SELLING GAME

3 MONTHS	6 MONTHS	1 YEAR	2 YEARS	5 YEARS
Explore 6 selling courses	Adapt & create 20 games & role plans	Select 4 assistants and train	Test-market direct mail assn w 4 different concerns	Franchise operation
Get brochures	Try out materials thru speaking engagements —dept stores —universities —women's groups	Teach 2 courses w all materials	Continue collecting testimonials	
Sign up for 2 courses	Start mailing list	Edit materials	Get publicity	
Read 10 books on sales	Watch for talent at speaking engagements	Explore associations —Sales Execs Club —Natl Org Women —Natl Assn Female Execs —Am. Financial Bus. Women		
Visit special business library. Consult librarian for best books.	Collect 20 testimonials	Start publicity file		
Set aside every Fri. for exploratory interviews. See 4 people connected w field each month	Hold 3 discussion sessions w women who have attended speeches, for feedback			
Have Judith explore 6 specific pitches, e.g., Tupperware, Arthur Murray, Avon, est, Berlitz	Invite 15 key women representing groups for idea generation			
Start file of techniques	Get lawyer			
Start bank acct.				

or four times out of five now have a set of odds—statistics—that applies to them. Translating further: If you're looking for a new job in a relatively crowded woman's field—real estate, acting, art, writing, public relations—your statistics may be that you'll win one time for every thirty jobs you go after. In less crowded areas, if you go counter to the traffic or gain the assistance of a partner, you'll enhance your statistics. Viewing the number of wins out of the number of tries as a statistic takes the emotion out of the rejections that are inevitable in any "game" and leaves you with something you can work with on a realistic and productive basis.

I'll give you an example. In my company the odds have changed over the last twelve years. It used to be that for every eight proposals we sent out, we could count on winning one job. Now our closure statistic is one job for every four proposals. So we strategize. As a company with a goal of forty projects a year, we must write 160 proposals in order to win. And when our proposal list gets too short, we go to work on an interim goal of lengthening the list, because no matter what, one out of four proposals will come through.

You can set realistic goals by looking at your own statistics. Count up the number of appointments you have made over the last two years, and the number of closures: one out of four, twenty, or whatever. That's your realistic statistic at this point. Work with it as such.

Beating the Statistical Competition

The people in our exercise who went counter to prevailing traffic won by improving their competitive odds. They could see they were in a crowded field, and therefore selected an area where there was more space. In career terms, the strategy is the same as the one used by a former workshop student, Ellie.

Ellie is in her mid-thirties, a brunette with huge dark eyes, very introspective, enormously gifted and at the same time extremely pragmatic. She has always been very serious about succeeding in her field, which is graphic design. She told me, "I could see that I was in a heavily overpopulated field. Everybody and his brother and sister is a graphic designer. I thought, 'It's madness to vie with a whole world full of designers. The thing to do is carve out a special need that only I and maybe a few others can fill.' I wanted to be different, to have a competitive edge. It happens that I was educated in South America and am fluent in the languages there. I also am keyed into the tastes and mores of both North and South America. So I figured, that's the special advantage I have over most other designers here. Furthermore, this is an age of specialists and business people like to feel they have a specialist all their own. The thing for me to do is weave my bi-American specialty together with graphic design and sell that to the buyers it would especially benefit. I studied the marketplace and found that there is a sizable number of Americans whose business it is to manufacture products for export to Brazil. So I went after them. I sold them on my knowledge of South American tastes and my ability to create designs Brazilian consumers would buy. I had practically no competition and I must say, I have the field practically to myself."

Studying the Marketplace

It is vital to find out everything you can about the field you're interested in before as well as while you're active in it. Thorough advance research will guide you as to whether or not the field is for you in the first place, and provide the information you'll need in order to know how to succeed.

Since we're talking about researching your goal, let's say that you think you'd like to go into architecture, or perhaps public relations or direct sales, but you know too little about the field to be sure it's for you. One excellent way to find out is by talking to a lot of people who are in various aspects of the field. Say it's direct sales. Give yourself a short-term goal of asking ten people who sell something what different types of direct sales exist. Find out what kinds of products or services are sold that way in your area, which of the fields are crowded and which are not. Use business libraries, government agencies, the Chamber of Commerce, directories, every source you can find. Dig in and discover what prerequisites you would need in order to break in: special training, a college degree, a car, a strong body. Don't be reticent about inquiring into every detail that flashes through your mind. Ask somebody if you can follow him or her around for a day, to observe at firsthand what its like to be in a particular field. People enjoy helping other people, sharing their knowledge and presenting informed points of view. Ask enough questions of enough people and you will gain an idea of the options that are available, and which ones are attractive to you.

Chances are when you wrote down your major motivation you thought about or wrote down a second motivation as well. It's all right, as long as you were honest about what is most important to you. There's nothing wrong in having a secondary, less urgent drive as long as you know which one is the stronger force, and as long as both are genuine. It's the masked desire that's the troublemaker.

Planned Partnerhood

Whether you're role-playing, laboring through the search for your goal, trying to make and hew to tough-sounding commitments, or need ideas and a pep talk, having a partner is one of the most powerful methods you can use for success. It's like the familiar buddy system you used when you were learning to swim, when you and another person were charged with watching out for each other's welfare. Only the career-building partner system goes far beyond the swimmer's. Unless you are a constitutional loner—very highly motivated, experienced, and disciplined—I urge you to adopt the method.

With a buddy, or partner, to listen and talk to, you can exchange information, add to your own experiences, get feedback, support, analysis, critiques, and advice. You can slice through confusion, digression, and depression. A partner will help you stay on goal and on schedule. Most of us are simply not sufficiently self-directed to manage all of this solo, or to see ourselves as others see us. We need the anchor of reporting to another person who will keep our minds and our efforts channeled in the direction we've chosen.

Make a Contract

The partner you select can be a friend or not, and preferably should come from the same area of expertise as yours so you can understand each other's problems and provide useful mutual assistance. He or she should be someone whose judgment you respect and who respects yours, so there will be productive interplay. The two of you should contract to meet formally and at regular intervals—once or twice a month, perhaps. Your first meeting may be to define your goals and discuss their reality, with subsequent meetings devoted to reviewing your progress toward those goals. When you miss the fact that you'd strayed from your purpose, been vague about strategy, or laissez faire about precious time, it's your partner's job to spot what's happening and give you the feedback and constructive advice by which you can work through to what you want. You, of course, will do the same in return. As in all good things connected with selling, you both win.

I've watched the system work well time after time. By creating a responsibility outside yourself, having somebody to report to and to be supportive when you're in doubt or fear, you automatically enhance your career power.

Joan and Elaina are extraordinary examples of how successful a partnership can be. They'd met at a workshop, when both were ripe to move on to new fields. Joan was a therapist, Elaina a marketing consultant. You must be thinking as they did at first, "But there's nothing in common here. How could they help each other?" Their commonality was that both were competent professionals, both wanted to expand their spheres and, as females, both felt the need for support from a peer. As it often turns out, the variations in their background proved complementary: What need or ability one lacked, the other had. The combination proved both stimulating and creative.

The contract Joan and Elaina wrote with one another called for them to meet at lunch every two weeks. Joan recalls, "When we met, we each had a one- and a five-year plan. We talked about these. We talked for twelve hours, in fact, using a tape recorder. When we reviewed what had been said, we realized that we could help each other stay on goal if we met and talked regularly. It was obvious we had a great mutual respect for each other's intelligence and ability to get jobs done. So we wrote out a contract whereby we'd be each other's kick-in-the-pants partner. In it, we agreed to assist one another in every way possible to accomplish her goals, even if it meant phoning each other every single day just to nag, 'Have you done this, have you met that goal?' We spelled it all out.

"Elaina's first project in the contract was to make twenty calls within the first two-week period and to accomplish a list of five specific goals. Mine read similarly. At our lunch meetings, we discussed our lists of goals and checked off whether we'd adhered to our time frames. We refined some of our original plans and worked out realistic strategies to implement them. Digressions, ramblings, and vagueness were disallowed per contract, and barrages of questions such as, 'Exactly how will you do this? By what date?' kept us both thinking clearly and in specifics.

"We got so much done in the first three months it was incredible. So we wrote out additional contracts, to maintain the enormously productive interchange of help. At the end of six months we found we'd completed all the goals we'd set down in our one-year plans. It was really remarkable. Elaina told me that just knowing that on Friday she'd have to sit down with me and review her goals and purposes, and compare that with how she used her time, really made her exquisitely aware of staying on purpose. We gave each other total support; that and our very 'oppositeness' gave an energy and freshness to everything we did.

"All this time each of us had been working separately toward organizational work, counseling women.

One day, we looked at the success we'd had with our partnership and said, 'This method works so wonderfully, why don't we join forces and teach it to other women so they can improve their professional and personal lives as we have?' We incorporated as Resource Center and the results have been more gratifying than I can say. We provide peer support that develops skills and enhances creativity and, perhaps most importantly, gives women the opportunity to learn from the experiences of others."

The partners-now-entrepreneurs still work on the premise of their original contract, reviewing it formally every three months, eliminating what doesn't work and polishing what does. They are one of the best examples I know of how support from someone who knows your fields, cares about your progress, and is willing to give advice can help you advance in your career.

You Are Not Alone

The buddy system is worth its weight in restaurant bills if meeting regularly with a partner helps you to make commitments. On your own, without a partner to monitor and assist you, the scariness of putting yourself on the line is apt to put you off—and the result is that you coast and drift, never getting anywhere. That's something that happens to many women, so don't feel it's shameful. Working together with somebody will help banish your fear.

Once you're committed to the idea of commitment, there's still work to be done. You must not only plot what your future will be five years from now, but also figure out how you'll reach that goal.

I can hear your mind clicking: "How do I do that? I don't even know who'll be president in five years, much less what my own campaign and strategy should be." You have a point, and if you also have a partner you have a way you can get on a course.

Make believe. Yes, you keep hearing that fantasy has no place in the selling game, but there are times when visions of sugar plums can be used creatively. It's the purposefully imaginative "What-if" springboard that has launched brilliant inventions—"What if a thin wire of tungsten were connected to carbon"; great novels—"What if three men were to use the Paris sewers to elude the *flics*"; and great sales ideas—"What if we hired women to sell kitchenware to other women by arranging parties in their homes."

More Role-Playing with Your Partner

Just as role-playing helped you uncover a hidden agenda in the last chapter, role-playing with a partner can help you see whether or not you are on track. In this case, the role-playing might more appropriately be called What-if-fing, but its purpose is the same—to help you see what is truly possible and to keep you on track.

Paula Partner: What if this were five years from now and what if you had sold yourself into a position at the top of your dream world. What would you be?

You: I'd be editor of a national magazine.

Paula Partner: What kind of magazine? What is its editorial theme? Who are its readers?

You: It's a beautifully illustrated magazine about food, wine, and travel. It's for a very select, affluent, sophisticated audience of men and woman.

Paula Partner: OK. Picture where you are and describe the scene. Who is with you? Why? What are you doing? What is the other perso doing? Give me all the details.

You: I'm in my private office at a large whit Lucite desk. I'm wearing the most magni icent *au courant* designer outfit you eve laid eyes on. The room is handsomely ca peted and exquisitely decorated. Produ samples and literature are arranged i cabinets along one wall, and a series of im maculate white files fills another. A youn woman is in the room with me, and I an directing her to update and recategoriz the filing system, and please to have i done by Wednesday.

Paula Partner: And you're smiling. Now tell me, wha would you have to do in the next si months, starting tomorrow, to attain th nirvana you've just described? Be specific If I've told you once I've told you a thou sand times, wishing and hoping don' count. Is there somebody you know wh can help you in some way?

You: Yes. I'll go see Max Mogul, an editor I now write for. He knows everybody in th magazine publishing field and could giv me information as well as introductions t other people who could help.

Paula Partner: That's a good resource and I'm proud o you for knowing right off the bat that yo have to build all the contacts you can, t get where you're going. Now think hard what else would you need?

You: Money. I'd have to start building a back- log of people who've shown an interest ir publishing and a willingness to invest in it.

Paula Partner: How would you prove to your investors that you have what it takes to run a magazine?

You: They'd want proof that I have knowledge, experience, and talent, so I'd start adding to my credentials by writing more articles about food, wine, and travel. I'd also get myself on some existing mastheads as a consultant or contributing editor.

Paula Partner: It's a good, clear plan. Have you thought about what you'd have to give up to get what you want?

You: There would be certain costs, but I consider them trade-offs. I couldn't travel with my husband on his sales trips, as he likes me to do, or take courses for a degree in drama, a project that's been in the back of my mind for years.

Paula Partner: You have to decide which is most important: being an independent editor of a prestigious magazine, serving your husband's needs, or taking courses in an avocational interest.

You: Personal issues are important, but I want that magazine editorship more than anything else and I'm willing to give up what I have to and accept the trade-offs without feeling guilty.

Name anything you'd like to achieve, within the boundary of reality, and play out the five-year What-if fantasy for yourself. The only rule is, you must be very specific throughout. And the follow-up is—follow up!

The Mentor Method

Hand in hand with the idea of partnering is the concept of mentoring. You've probably had mentors all your life: teachers, relatives, colleagues—people who have done what you're doing before you, who can see your strengths and help you develop them.

A woman I know who now does information processing and analysis for major corporations tells me that she has always been aware of having a number of mentors to whom she could turn at any time. "One mentor who's been very important to me was the person who labeled what I was doing and told me what business I could get into. He was a man I had hired in a previous job to come in and do training. He watched me dealing with people before and during the meeting, and said, 'You have very good training skills.' He began labeling things that he saw me doing as a whole other set of professional skills. I'd thought they were just nice personal skills, hostessing and planning abilities, until he put wholly different labels on them: facilitating, helping people become self-directed. He was right, and I knew it. He then told me where there was training available in workshops and helped me look in a catalog and pick one out. Then, when I was in graduate school he hired me to do some co-training work with him. He referred me to two other places, so I helped put myself through graduate school. That's really significant. He literally took me on as an apprentice. My sense is that he in fact saw himself as my mentor. He took great pleasure in teaching me. He has an ego that flowers under the eyes of an apprentice. He likes to be looked up to. As soon as I outgrew the apprentice role, our relationship cooled substantially."

Help Is Everywhere

Finding a mentor or a partner is not always easy. You may find that you're in a place or phase when the right individuals just aren't available to you. All is not lost. If there's a support group where you live, join it. It's a perfect place to find the help you need, and you can begin to structure your own network. If you're really on your own, you can still create a support system by getting help in one area from one person, adding to it with help in another area from a second person, and so on. The object is to have wise and helpful people assist you in setting and reaching specific goals, so you can have the satisfaction of accomplishment: the knowledge that you have won at what you set out to do.

Reality: *It's hard to get from here to there alone. Find someone "on goal" to share your journey.*

4

Organizing for Success

Now that you have learned that reaching goals does not happen miraculously, you also have to face the fact that a lot of organization is involved any time you want to get from Point A to Point B.

The time to get yourself organized is not after you are halfway submerged in a project, but before you begin the actual work. The first step in organizing yourself is to learn to master your time.

Time must be handled on both a day-to-day and an ongoing basis, and always with realistic flexibility. If you feel that you can't handle Tuesday's list of things to do because you woke up feeling miserable, recognize that you won't perform well that day and defer whatever you can till Wednesday. If your quarterly "corporate review" of your goal sheet shows that changes should be made, make them. Nowhere is it written that there is merit in being rigid and unimaginative.

A powerful technique for staying in charge of time is to make yourself accountable to someone else. Very few people are so disciplined that they can keep on goal and on schedule without an outside "conscience" as a goad. Use your partner as your goad and write a contract with her that will encourage and force you to adhere to the timetables you've set.

Your Time Is Your Money

Mastering time is the hardest, most dismaying work in the world for some people. But if you're going to be successful, you have to learn to use time, instead of letting it use you. There are only twenty-four hours in each day, and time is a limited, therefore precious commodity.

One way to conquer the tyranny of time is to put a dollar value on it. What are you worth—$75 an hour? Then taking time out of your day to type reports or do laundry doesn't make sense. You could hire somebody else to do it at $7 or $15 an hour. That would be a sound, pragmatically realistic investment; by making it you'd retain the full value of your own time.

At $75 an hour or however you price yourself, you're going to want to make every hour count. An excellent method of keeping track is to get into the habit of keeping time sheets. Block off each time sheet into segments and write into each segment the time spent, what you did, and for which client or customer: "Sales call, ABC Co." "Corresp. re Blank account." "Rsch job market in Akron." In addition to keeping you productive, time sheets help keep you solvent. They are a cost accounting system: At the end of each day or week, when you add up the time you devoted to each specific project, you will se immediately where your profit and loss has been. Som sample time sheets follow on pages 60–61.

The Importance of Priorities, Shifting or Otherwise

There you are with a goal date looming fast and you'r nowhere near ready to meet it. It's alarming. Time ha somehow gone highballing past and you are frantic. Wha went wrong? Where did your grip slip?

The best way to keep prime targets in sight is t keep them in sight. Literally. On lists like your Goa Sheet. And the best way to keep first things first an prevent ditsy projects from gobbling your time and en ergies is to make fresh lists of your mini-range project every day. The very act of writing things down in 1, 2, order forces you to think—and to plan. And the time yo spend on advance planning is a gift to yourself: It wi shorten the time you spend later on performance.

Schedule each day as it comes. Each priority need continuous reassessment, as needs and situations chang constantly. If there's a store opening up and you're in th business of selling Product X, you can't be indentured t yesterday's priority. You have to drop everything and ge to the new store, fast and first.

List each day's appointments in your diary: 10:30 conference, 2:00 meeting, 4:00 interview. And make a second list of things to do, in order of their importance or urgency. The top of your To Do list should be things that will take you closer to your goal. If the rest of the list runs too long and can't be completed, review it and eliminate, postpone, or get somebody else to take care of the inconsequential activities, the things you don't really have to do. Otherwise you'll waste irreplaceable time chasing up and down dead-end alleys. Focus on what needs doing now, or you'll be like my aunt who never has the right thing to wear. Every time Aunt Rose goes out for a new pair of shoes to match the suit she has to wear next week, she's seduced by the goodies in Lingerie—flits from there to the distractions of Kitchenware—stops at Toiletries for a pinch of this and a nibble at that. She never gets to Shoes at all. You know the type? Aunt Rose is one of those lovable, well-meaning, slightly frumpy scatter-brains, and it's a blessing she doesn't need to earn a living.

Focus on First Things First

We're all tempted by things that can tug us off goal. A friend told me about a near-fatal instance of priority side-tracking that came along while she was studying to be a theatrical attorney and sometime producer. One day, with bar exams a mere six months away, a man named Mr. Wonderful called and said he was backing a Broadway show and would she like to start right away as producer. Of course her instant reaction was "Fabulous! I would love it. Here's a beautiful opportunity, dropped right into my lap." Then she realized that if she waded into producing a show, she couldn't finish studying for the bar and would be throwing away her primary goal of becoming a theatrical attorney. Sanity intervened in time and the priorities became indisputably clear. She called Mr. Would-Be Wonderful, explained the situation, and offered to find somebody for him who was immediately available to produce his show. She also stored his name in her growing collection of contacts. Later, when the law

DAILY TIME SHEET

Date:

(Advertising Consultant)

		Hours														
Job #	Job Description	8	9	10	11	12	1	2	3	4	5	6	7	8	Totals	Billing Amount
CS 684	Clerk Stores Client conference															
AS 685	Astor Shoes Copy for catalog															
CR 27	Chain Restaurants Casting TV commercials															
Staff	New business conference															

WEEKLY TIME SHEET

(Boutique Owner)

Week of:

Project	Mon.	Tues.	Weds.	Thurs.	Fri.	Sat.	Total Hours	Comments
				Hours per day				
Serving customers							6	Line up extra help for Xmas season
Stockroom							1	Check total at end of week—consider hiring stockboy
Lunch with supplier							1½	
Correspondence & billing							2	See accountant
Mtg. with ad agency							1	

degree is in her possession and it's time to get into th production side of show business, she'll have that card a a reminder of a person who likes to put money int shows.

The Mañana Trip

There's another caveat to build into your list-makin habit. Postponing non-urgent things to do translates, fo some people, to falling into the procrastination trap. It's a trip on the tumbrel, a killer, but it's one frailty you ca keep in its place. Here are some constructive habits t substitute for the counterproductive urge to procrastinate.

1. Slice the chore that seems onerous into small, digestible portions and tackle one slice at a time. It will take the "overwhelming" out of the largest task.

2. Whittle down your habit of procrastinating by taking on the tasks you've been putting off, one at a time. Completing one "unpleasant" chore a day will give you that exhilarating feeling of accomplishment, won't hurt a bit, and will get you into the habit of tackling what needs to be done without alibiing it under the rug.

3. Force yourself to make more lists: two for each job you're procrastinating. On List A, write the reasons why you're not doing whatever you're not doing, and on List B write down the benefits that will accrue if you get the job done. List A will look silly: "It might be boring." "I can't think of what to wear when I do it." List B will look sensationally attractive: "I'll earn $150." "It will be educational." And, surely a major reward, "The job will be done and over with."

4. Blend desire with duty. On a rainy morning when you have thirty phone calls you must complete that day and you don't want to get out of bed, satisfy both needs. Be nice to yourself. Bring the phone and coffeepot in next to your bed and start call number one. The people you're phoning will never know where you're calling from, and you will have gotten started despite your lallygagging, by taking one small step at a time.

As somebody's said, "If procrastination is your problem, don't put off doing something about it."

Research—The Most Important Time-saver

Research is the activity that all successful persons use to avoid wasting their precious hours and efforts on activities that are not feasible. Through research you learn what is and what is not possible *before* launching into a full-scale attack on a project. Research also makes you more efficient when you do act—and efficiency always saves time.

With research properly done, you never have to succumb to the useless fluttering that comes from not being sure where you are going or what your basis for acting is. So many activities—and even goals, for that matter—can and should be avoided because they are inappropriate or won't get you where you want to go. The best way to know what to avoid is to do your research in advance.

Whether you plan to find a job, get a raise, start a new business, or increase your rates, you'll save yourself enormous amounts of time if you dig in and get all the facts before you begin.

Organizing Your Research

As you gather more and more information, and particularly as that information begins to translate into sales, you will want to develop a storage system for your research and sales materials. Keeping data in systemized files is one of the shortest cuts to professionalism. In fact, it's essential. Whether you are in business for yourself or are with a company that has its own systems, you'll always need to be able to put your hands on specific information quickly and accurately.

Organizing Job Files

One storage system that is a must for the well-organized professional is the Job File. Don't wait until you have garnered ten jobs to set up your Job File; start it the minute you get your first job so you'll always be in control. Here are some guidelines for creating a Job File; alter them as necessary to fit your personal needs and working methods.

1. Assign a number to each prospect, client, or customer you acquire:

ABC Co. = 1
DEF, Inc. = 2
GHI Assoc. = 3

2. Assign a second number to each project for each of the prospects, clients, or customers:

ABC Co.: 11, 12, 13, etc.
DEF, Inc.: 21, 22, 23, etc.
GHI Assoc.: 31, 32, 33, etc.

After a period of time, those codes could look like this:

ABC Co.: 1431
DEF, Inc.: 2210
GHI Assoc.: 3119

You can use your master code in a number of ways:

a. To identify a project's deadline.
b. To identify a project's work status ("In progress," "Canceled," "Completed").
c. To identify a project's estimated and actual cost.
d. For billing purposes (you can augment the master code with a file folder system: one file for each project, coded appropriately—"193" for the ABC Co.'s October project, for example—will supply all the time, out-of-pocket expenses, and fee information you need to get your billing out quickly).

Assume Your Memory Is Rotten

Aside from the fact that you should be writing down everything you learn about yourself, your career, and your clients, you will also rely heavily on a filing system to store this information. Files on clients, for example, should contain information on deadlines for projects, the work status of projects, billing information, and estimates and costs. No matter how important the client or the job, do not assume that you will remember important or unimportant information. Assume that you will remember nothing, make and file accurate records—and you will never have to suffer the embarrassment of having to call a client to ask him to repeat information you should have firmly in hand.

Reality: *Successful selling is being well-organized and covering all of the bases all of the time.*

5

Total Career Power: getting it and using it

> A young woman recently came in to see me for a job. There's no doubt in my mind that she'll go places one of these days. She's very bright and talented, and her enthusiasm is great. But she's not willing to be trained right now. She's in too much of a hurry. She won't invest the time and effort required to learn the basics of a job she wants. So she compensates for her lack of knowledge by trying to fake it, which puts her into oversell. I simply couldn't hire her.

As this example shows, the mistake too many women make is in thinking that they can make it on enthusiasm alone, or that because they have personal style or professional expertise, they will naturally succeed in selling. They think, "I'm so good at what I do it'll sell itself. What I'm offering is really terrific and naturally people are going to come and seek it out." Or, "I'm so loaded with energy and zest I can talk anybody into anything, even if I don't know very much about the product or service I'm talking about." Often such feelings are a natural result of the thought and planning that goes into choosing a goal you want to follow. You get so enthusiastic over your plans that you forget the need to assess carefully what you have to sell, what you will need to get your career off the ground and moving toward the ultimate goal—success.

To be sure, expertise and enthusiasm are two qualities you cannot do without. But they are totally interdependent on each other, and on a third vital quality as well: the ability to sell. Professional expertise, positive outlook, and selling ability—the three operating as a totality—is the dynamic that can make a person be truly successful. It is the framework of mature professionalism, the structure whose elements are inextricably linked. Weakness in one diminishes strength in the others; strength in all three underlies every success.

To simplify what total career power is, let's compare it with something with which you are already familiar: the child's board game, Chutes and Ladders. The game, you'll recall, consists of a series of squares, a pair of dice, and markers representing the players. You move around the board according to what turns up on each throw of the dice, sometimes advancing many squares ahead on the ladder and sometimes slipping back down the chutes all the way back to START. The marker that represents *you* can be in the shape of a perfect pyramid. If each side is as tall and as strong as the others, it will move along wherever you place it. But what if it were lopsided, with one or two of its sides weak? The marker would wobble on the board so that you couldn't move along from space to space and play out the game to WIN.

In your career, just as in Chutes and Ladders, you need a balanced pyramid or you'll keep falling off the board.

Let's analyze the pyramid playing-piece that is essential for career power. Within the center of its three sides is *you:* your persona, your ethics, your style and personality. These are qualities that can be studied in others and nurtured in yourself, but they are personal characteristics and nobody can teach them to you. Nor is there any right or wrong to them per se; what's right is what's comfortable for you. Your style may be subdued or energetic. You may be maternal or commanding. One is no better or more effective than another; style is simply the personal flavor you impart through the manner in which you communicate your thoughts.

Elizabeth has observed her personal style change through the years, and become enhanced by the strengthening of her professional, selling, and attitudinal powers. She characterizes herself as informal and straightforward, and feels that in some cases her style has been "the difference that sells." She says, "When I first started in business I was very loath to reveal anything of myself. I'd never open up and speak about *me.* You could even see it in my body language: I'd sit hunched over with my knees pressed together and my arms hugging my chest. Let a client ask something as simple as 'Do you have brothers and sisters?' and I'd scurry away, verbally—then wonder why it took me so long to find out about *them.* I've found, though, that the more business contacts I've made and the more strangers I've talked with, the more open I've become about myself. I show my cards right away now: who I am, what my interests are, things I was so concealing about. I let my personality come through, and it helps us both. One way I do this is by asking questions.

For example, when I go to somebody's office on a sales call, I'll look around and pick up a clue to ask something personal about. 'Oh, did you take these photographs? Is photography your hobby? It's mine, too.' I'll go into it a little bit: 'I do my own color processing, do you? I picked up a tip recently from a commercial photographer that you might like to use . . .' I find that twenty minutes or so of that sort of opening conversation lets you get something going with a total stranger, and gets them to communicate with you . . . even trust you. It's an informal entry that gets us both off the anxiety-centered topic of why I'm making the sales call. It puts us both more at ease and lets me find out a bit more about the other person before I get down to business. Being direct and honest in manner, and giving them something to relate to, builds their confidence in me."

Inez says her caretaking style has evolved from having been the oldest of four children. "I did a lot of training and explaining things to people who were younger or less experienced than I was, and I've transferred that experience to my career as an adult and find it very enjoyable. Growing up as the oldest, I got a kick out of being the expert and the one who'd done it before—the one who was explaining to somebody else. I still do. There's a direct relationship between that childhood feeling and my style in selling to people now. The experience has carried over into my becoming a person who is like the mentor, the mother, the rock people can rely on. I think everybody is looking for a parent—a mommy or daddy who will take responsibilities and lead them through what they are doing. And I think that's how people view me now."

Your style is as individual as your fingerprint. It is your life experience, your environment, your values.

How it enlarges your capacity to succeed depends on the powers you surround it with—your career powers.

The Base of Your Career-Power Pyramid: Professional Expertise

> I've always tried to get things by just selling my eagerness and my willingness to work. And yet, how far have I gotten?

Professional expertise is being very good at what you do, and having the credentials to prove it. The better you are at what you do, the stronger and broader that side of your career-power pyramid is. Whether you're a doctor, a fund-raiser, a hairdresser, or seller of somebody else's product or service, unless you are knowledgeable in your area of expertise, you've nothing to sell.

Reality: *If you don't know what you are doing, you are just faking it. You have to know what you are selling.*

Take Sylvia. She's a travel agent. She possesses enormous selling skills. One of those people who can get Eskimos to buy ice—once. I know, because Sylvia once sold my husband and me on a summer vacation in Vermont that we'll never forget—or repeat. She called us up, effervescing with what she had to offer: "This place is *you!* It's absolutely magnificent. There's an incredible beach. I'm looking at a picture of it right now and I can see the most fabulous shells; you could make a collection of them. And there's a gorgeous panorama in back of the lake, with trees sweeping across hills that rise straight to the sky. No question, you're going to have the best week of your lives here."

When we arrived, we learned that everything Sylvia'd said was true; it was what she hadn't researched and didn't tell us that hurt. The place was a swarm of mosquitoes. The furniture was impossibly rickety. And the lake bottom was so rocky you couldn't swim. It was obvious that Sylvia had never visited the place or made valid inquiries; she'd relied on brochures and let it go at that. She oversold us into that week in Vermont, but she'll never get us—or our friends—as customers again.

Sylvia has enthusiasm coming out of her pores, gets so excited every time she makes a pitch that her fervor is contagious and people are swept along in the storm of her belief in what she's selling. She is unable to achieve a true career of continuing success and her sales amount to occasional one-shots because she is faking it. She hasn't done more than skim the surface of the travel business, knows only smatterings about destinations and deals, sells what sounds good at the moment without any substantiation. She lacks professional expertise and until she fills in that gap and strengthens that side of her pyramid, she will always be selling blue sky. Once.

What Sylvia needs to do is take the time to bolster her expertise by attending workshops, business courses, seminars. She could also join forces with a consortium of experts in her field who could augment her knowledge. She should read up on everything to do with the travel business and get out and experience travel packages for herself. And she can gain the expertise she needs without losing the momentum she has going for her. She can keep right on selling travel and improving her professionalism while she works, if she is willing to sacrifice a few evenings with her friends and family. At this stage, it is essential to make a priority of strengthening that side of her career power.

Career Power Continued: Confidence, (Side Two of Your Pyramid)

Confidence, or a positive outlook about yourself and your abilities, is the second important element in Total Career Power. Many women are weak in this area because they've been taught not to present themselves positively or forcefully, and because they have such overwhelming fear of being rejected. Frequently, as in Marjorie's case, the absence of a positive outlook is a complete hindrance.

Marjorie has what Sylvia lacks: professional expertise. Still she's not successful. Marjorie designs children's clothing. Her ideas are fresh, functional, fun, great looking—and ought to sell like hula hoops, nationwide. Yet the samples sit in her studio, collecting cobwebs and going nowhere. Marjorie's problem is twofold. She lacks confidence, doesn't believe in herself; and she's afraid that if she tries to sell her designs she'll be turned down. She has admitted, "I never step out fully, just halfway. I'll sit in my studio and work out something really nice, a design I feel good about. And then I'll let my mind take over and start to see myself being rejected. I'll imagine myself going into a buyer's office and being scrutinized, and feeling inferior. I can hear the 'No.' So my beautiful designs just sit here, because I just never have the guts to take them out and sell them."

What Marjorie *could* do is go the route of having somebody else, an agent or rep, take over the sales end. In which case she'd be a behind-the-scenes person all her life, turning out nice little designs, not being in the swing of the marketplace, and managing to sell a few items now and then.

A great part of confidence can be learned through a

set of practical exercises and techniques, and Marjorie can even out her lopsided career-power pyramid by attending support groups such as assertiveness training workshops or a human potential seminar that will strengthen her positive feelings about herself. She could take adult continuation courses, and read the tons of books and articles that are so helpful to people who are looking for guidance in learning confidence. Through these efforts she could begin to overcome her fears and self-doubt, and develop the attitude that says, "I can do it and I will do it." With a positive attitude about herself she will be better able to pick up the phone, make appointments with buyers, get out there and ask for what she wants. These steps are scary. It takes a lot of practical commitment and self-determination to correct the wobbly playing-piece that is preventing Marjorie from moving from talented dreamer to successful designer.

Reality: *It is not written in stone that making changes is easy.*

Wilma is another talented person whose outlook held her back. She worked very hard and for a long time so that she could move ahead from being fearful and not getting results into giving her playing piece the power she needed to move up the ladder to WIN.

Wilma was fired from her first job as art director for a children's book publisher because, in her own words, "I was not consistent in what I did. Some of my design solutions were good, some were not; you couldn't count on consistently good results. I found out later the reason for it. It was because I was so afraid—not that the work wouldn't be accepted, but that *I* wouldn't be. I'd completely confused my goals, if it could be said that I had any. I didn't, and that was part of my problem. I realized what was going on when I got fired: that I really hadn't been working with awareness, and how could I do good work 100 percent of the time and be effective if I wasn't aware of what I was doing? Being fired and realizing that I was out of contact with myself frightened me further. I spoke with a dear friend about it, and her advice was to see a therapist. She said, 'Wilma, you have a great talent, but your work is not consistent and neither is your behavior. Go and get help.' It was the greatest thing I ever did; it made everything clear. It let me acknowledge my own professional talent and think, 'It's good. It's what I want to sell; what I can and will sell. It's what I can learn how to use properly, now that I'm aware it's not *me* people might reject, but my designs.' Gaining that consciousness of myself was a long slow process, but now I know how to use what I have. Before, I was like Sleeping Beauty. A prince was going to discover me, I'd wake from his kiss and, magically, everything would be all right. I just was not awake to what I wanted or what I had to give, so I never followed through or succeeded."

Almost everybody doubts him or himself, and is scared at some time. Helen, who once had a problem with shyness but developed the confidence and expertise that allowed her to move forward nonetheless, capsulizes the attitudinal aspect of her fourteen-year career this way. "Before I began selling, I was very doubtful that I could do it. Or that I would enjoy it. Once I got into it and learned how to do it, my attitude changed radically. It was very different from what I'd expected. I'd thought that I would have to push harder than I did, and that I'd be very uncomfortable dealing with people. The two were interconnected in my mind, and I just didn't think I'd be any good at all. But getting out there and *doing* it has taken me way past that attitude. And getting beyond those feelings not only has made selling easier, it has made it pleasurable for me. I've gone from shyness to enjoying the opportunity of meeting interesting people. You know how sometimes you find somebody you just enjoy talking to, and even when you don't, you sort of file that person away as an interesting character? I can do that now, freely.

"The one thing I've learned is that positive feelings and confidence in yourself keep building. When you take a chance and get the thing that you want, reach the goal you've set, you get a strength from that. You look at it and say, 'I got that. If I can do that, I can do this.' And then you go on to the next goal and say, 'I got A and B, now I can get C. I'm just going to go for it.' You keep building and building. People can give you the traditional arguments about why you shouldn't do what you want to do, and why you'll never succeed at it because you're a woman, but you're the only one who can prove to yourself whether you can or cannot get what you want. I think the important part is making the effort. Even if it doesn't turn out the exact way you want it to, you did it. You set that goal and you worked at it with the idea that you could win it."

One third of selling is having the confidence that you are going to succeed in whatever you try. Confidence gives power to your career playing-piece.

Your Selling Ability: The Third Side of Your Pyramid

Now we come to Joanna. She is one of the best journalists you'll ever meet: a thorough researcher, a deft writer, conscientious about deadlines. As a free-lance reporter she's aces, and she knows it. Her attitude about herself and what she does is thoroughly upbeat. So there are two solid sides to her pyramid playing-piece: She has professional expertise and she is confident and optimistic. But Joanna has been looking for a job for nearly a year and at this point is blocked from ever getting anywhere because of the one skill she is missing: the ability to sell. The woman has no idea how to go about persuading people to want what she can give them.

The editor-in-chief of a suburban newspaper told me how Joanna's been operating. Right now, being editor of the paper's Living Pages is a job she wants so much she can taste it. It's a job she'll never get, despite her competence. What she did was walk into the editor's office and tell him how she was going to take over the show. Just like that. "Look," she as much as said, "you have a problem and you're incapable of handling it, so you'd better just turn it over to me." She approached the editor as if he were an idiot who didn't know what he was doing, and left neither of them with a way to win. Making her prospective employer wrong was fatal to Joanna's ambitions, because making somebody wrong is the cardinal sin in selling. She could have won him over, instead, by showing him how she could fit into his needs and existing organizational structure. She could have said, "Perhaps you have a problem and possibly I can help you in a number of ways that would fit into your structure." She could have won him over by asking questions, supporting his needs, getting his agreement, showing him he had something to win by buying her services.

The editor's response, to himself, was, "I need a team player here and this one's a takeover artist. I want someone in here who'll support what we're doing, someone I can rely on to follow my concepts and structure, and not fight me every step of the way. I wouldn't have her on my staff no matter how good she is."

Reality: *Selling is strategy—not takeover.*

Creating a win/win situation is one of the selling skills many women, like Joanna, need to learn. Success goes hand in hand with working cooperatively and constructively with other people's ideas, and with assessing situations ahead of time or at least on the spot instead of making assumptions. Among the myriad methods of acquiring the basic tenets of selling are reading books like this one and taking courses, then extracting the kernels that fit your needs best, to create a formula you are comfortable with. After all, *you* are always at the heart of your career playing-piece, and the one-size-fits-all formula doesn't exist that is comfortable for everybody.

In terms of selling ability and style, Pam is the flip side of Joanna. She knows very well the pitfalls of making another person wrong—any person, not just somebody she's selling to at the moment. She tells a story of having been invited to a dinner party given by the large realty firm she works for. At the time, she was in a stepping-stone phase of her career and was intent on getting a promotion very soon. She says, "There were a lot of executives at the party, people I wouldn't normally have had a chance to talk with. One of them was asking me questions about what I thought the company's weak spots were, how we could increase our sales. There *were* several things at the time that I thought were not right. For example, at the lower management level there wasn't enough organization behind the salespeople to let them function effectively. But I was in a funny position because I was working in the department we were talking about and what I said could place the blame on the sales manager's shoulders. I had to be very careful; I didn't want to make anybody else look bad, I wanted to keep the dialogue intellectual and not get onto any personal level, pointing the finger at anybody, because that's not what it was about. It was about business and we were talking about business. I had to think very carefully before I spoke, because even though I did want to get ahead in the company, I didn't want to get ahead on somebody else's back. It would surely boomerang; those things always do. That particular incident was a big learning experience for me in realizing the ramifications of what could possibly happen if you take a conversation a certain way. You have to think ahead of yourself all the time—when you're chatting, when you're making a real hard pitch, in every situation. You have to be direct and honest, and clear so everybody knows what you're saying. And you have to be careful not to create losers, because if you do, you'll be a loser, too, in the end."

Assess Your Career Power

How strong or how lopsided is your career-power pyramid? To get a picture of where you stand and what area needs the most work, give an honest evaluation of your three sides as they are at this very moment. Rate yourself on a scale of 1 to 10 as follows:

1–3: Needs improvement
4–6: Fair to good
7–10: Very good to excellent

I To evaluate your professional expertise:

1. Rate your credentials or education degrees

YOUR GAME PIECE

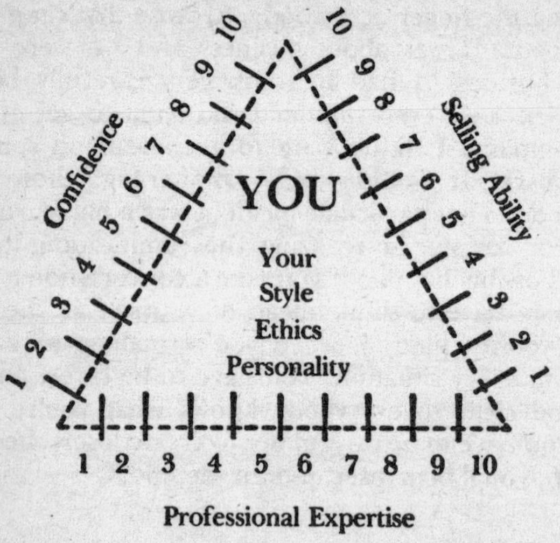

2. Rate your work experience in your field ______
3. Rate your life experience touching on your field ______
4. Rate how well you know your product ______

Total ______

Divide by 4 ______

II To evaluate your confidence:

1. Rate how confident you feel about your professional expertise ______
2. Rate how confident you feel with selling ______

3. Rate how clear and confident you are about your immediate goals _____
4. Rate how clear and confident you are about your long-range goals _____

Total _____

Divide by 4 _____

III To evaluate your selling ability:

1. Rate how well your product stacks up against the competition _____
2. Rate your ability to get leads _____
3. Rate your ability to make appointments _____
4. Rate your ability to tell your product story convincingly _____
5. Rate your ability to close a deal _____

Total _____

Divide by 5 _____

6

Three Little Words: the big three in selling

I can't stand rejection. I guess that's what keeps me from making the calls I know I should be making. I mean, there's a good chance the person will say No to me if I call. I think people should call me when they want something. They ought to know I do good work, and it's for sale.

You are going to hear one of three answers every time you sell, whether you are selling yourself, a product, or a service. The answers you'll hear will be Yes, No, or Maybe, and you'd better learn all you can about each because Yes, No, and Maybe will be the base you have to work from in selling. This chapter explains how to cope with each of the three answers.

Let's Hear It for "Yes"

If I ask you, "Which of the three words do you want most to hear?" you'll probably say what everybody says: Yes. You'll be absolutely right, of course. For anyone in selling, Yes is the best word ever invented. It's what you've been working to get: the agreement from someone to act on or buy what you have to offer. No question: a Yes is paradise gained—for most.

There are some people who have difficulty when they hear the word *Yes.* Tell them, "Yes, the job is yours," and they immediately start unselling. "How am I going to get a baby-sitter? Who'll fix my husband's supper? I can't possibly start for another two months." The problem is they're so sure nobody could really want them, they've foreseen only failure. The Yes takes them by surprise and they've no idea how to deal with it. The trouble with a lot of people who can't take Yes for an answer is they have a hidden agenda not to succeed and their whole attitude is built around No. Gina's story is typical.

Gina, The Painter Who Couldn't Take Yes

Since we've been living in the West Indies, I've been painting realistically, and for the past two years my theme has been tropical flowers. I did a series of twenty-four paintings, each one related to the other, and I loved having them around my studio. It was like having the outside inside. Recently my husband had to go to Florida on business, and I went along and set up appointments with Miami art dealers and gallery owners. I lucked out on the first try. A patron of mine had introduced me to a dealer whose tastes were similar to hers. In forty minutes the dealer had purchased three of my paintings and taken eight on consignment. She offered me $350 for each, and I grabbed at it. I was elated . . . until I walked out the door. Suddenly I felt depressed and upset. I had accepted her offer to purchase too quickly. I didn't know if $350 was a fair price, and worse, I was giving up my babies. The series was no longer complete; I didn't know if I'd done the right thing and I was pretty miserable. I stayed up all night and called the dealer first thing the next day, saying I wanted my paintings back. She became very agitated over my unprofessionalism, so I didn't make a definite appointment to go pick them up. I began calling my painter friends to ask what to do, though it was a little after the fact. I finally understood that the $350 was a fair price and, as one friend told me, what was wrong was that I was going through the feeling of having given birth and then watching the child leave home for the first time. I'll probably always have that feeling, but I can't hang on to everything I produce. They have to go out in the world.

What's the Worst Word You Can Hear?

You'll probably give the same answer most other people give, too, if I ask you, "What's the worst word of the three?": No. You'd prefer to hear Maybe because it seems to imply there's still hope. That's like the captain of the *Titanic* facing an iceberg and suggesting "Perhaps we might rearrange the furniture on the deck" . . . fantasy. The reality is, *Maybe* is the worst word you can hear.

I'll explain more about the perils of Maybe in a minute. First let's explore the value of a good resounding No. It *is* valuable. Not as good as a Yes, but light-years better than Maybe.

No Is a Word You Can Work With

> I was always somebody who felt more comfortable hearing Maybe than No, because then I could hold on to my fantasy about what might happen, and because it meant I didn't actually have to confront a No.

Imagine yourself in this scene: You've gone in to an interview with your goal clearly in mind and the facts concerning your product or service properly marshaled. You've spoken persuasively in terms of what you can do for the company and not what the company can do for you. You've given the interviewer your best, and his or her answer is—a dagger through the heart: No.

The reality is, No is not a dagger; it's a wonderful opportunity, one to take advantage of quickly. Rather than going berserk, losing your focus, and forgetting why you're there (do you know the feeling?), you react to the answer in a straight, collected manner. You are immune to the word *No* as a negative, and hear it instead as a door opener to questions you'll ask that can change No to Yes.

Notice, I said questions, not statements. You're inquiring, not attacking; respecting your interviewer's opinions; never making him or her wrong. Here is how you can use No to elicit information that can help you make the sale.

Interviewer: No, I don't see you for this particular job.
You: I see. Let me ask you a question. What qualifications would I need in order to come back and see you again in six months?

or

Interviewer: No, what you propose is out of the question at this time.
You: You say "at this time." Apparently you feel

there will be a time when we can talk about my proposal. Perhaps there's something else right now, an obstacle you haven't mentioned. Are delivery schedules a problem for you?

or

Your questions can reveal that you got a No simply because the other person didn't understand everything about what you were trying to sell them.

Interviewer: No. Your fabrics don't fit into my color scheme.

You: I notice that you like sunny colors. As a matter of fact, these fabrics come not only in the blues I showed you, but also in yellow. And I can get any of the other shades that tie in with yellow for you. Are you planning to do the whole house in those tones, or just this room?

The No you heard was not a loss. It was a wedge. It gave you a way to find out why he or she said No, and to get suggestions for alternate routes to your goal, other needs you might fill. It let you find out when or how it would be feasible to try the sale again. It let you make discoveries.

Changing No to Yes

> It doesn't bother me any more when somebody says No. I can just go and and get Yes somewhere else later on. And the No doesn't hurt because I know it's for the product I'm selling, not me personally.

Linda, a fashion coordinator, thought of a way to extend her expertise in grooming women to benefit large corporations by providing complete styling, from clothing and accessories to makeup and hairstyles as services for their employees. The employees would benefit from her help and so would the corporations, in terms of having better groomed, more poised employees. She made an appointment and presented her fashion package service to an airline company for their hostesses and reservations clerks. The immediate response was negative: "But you've never done a whole program for anybody before." Since it *was* her first attempt at providing total fashion coordination for a corporation, Linda was momentarily tempted to dodge the issue and fake her experience. Wisely, however, she faced the challenge honestly and said, "You're right. I haven't done this whole program for anybody else before, but I am confident the pieces fit. What I'm proposing is custom-tailored to your organization. It is based on my expertise in knowing what to do and how to do it, and I am certain that you will be pleased with the results in terms of employee morale and the image you present to your public. Let me tell you a way we can try it out without your having to make a large commitment right away."

What Linda did in this case history was change a No to a Yes by being forthright and positive, and by making it easy for her prospect to act.

A No Is Not a Loss, and It Isn't Forever

A No is not the end of the line; it is fertile soil you can seed so a Yes will blossom. Nor is No a battleground. When it's the correct answer, based on reality, you can accept it pleasantly, put it behind you, and go on to sell to the next person. A reality-based No has one highly desirable quality: It completes a cycle for you and lets you get on with your work. It's a definite answer, a conclusion to the project you are working on.

A No is nothing to get emotional about. It is not

somebody disliking you personally; it's just another statistic. Every selling job has statistics. You may need five contacts to connect on one interview, or your statistics may be that one of every four persons to whom you pitch your product will buy. So think of each No as another statistic: If you know you need to collect five Noes to get a Yes, then one more No merely puts you statistically closer to your goal.

A No is not fatal. It may represent temporary loss, but remember this: Nobody wins them all—and nobody loses them all, either.

There's one more thing a No is not. It is not your anxious mother or autocratic father barking, "No, don't touch this! No, don't do that!" You're not six years old now and you won't be sent to your room, so your mature response to No is to recognize your conditioned reflex as an old acquaintance perched on your shoulder. Acknowledge it. Tell it, "Hello, we've met before and I know what you're all about. For a moment you made me feel I was sinking, but now I'll just get on with what I know I can do."

Maybe Is the Worst Word in the Book

You may think Maybe is a lifeline, that as long as somebody hasn't said No, you have a chance. Not so. Maybe is a mire that can bog you down and lead nowhere. It's perilous territory to be ensnared in, and you'd best get out as quickly as possible.

A Maybe really is to put you off or get rid of you. Unless you reshape it to a definite Yes or No, it is a worthless answer you can't do a thing with. "Maybe we'll hire more people in February." "Maybe we could talk bout it sometime when you're in town again." "Maybe . . . I don't know." A Maybe leaves you in limbo, tranded, unable to move. You've no objections to anwer, no points to parry. The best thing, the only thing o do with Maybe is refuse to live with it any longer than ou have to.

Reality: Maybe *isn't opportunity knocking; it's the its.*

Two Kinds of Maybe's

There are two kinds of Maybe's. One is the *real* postoned decision, when the person you're selling to has a alid reason for delay. The real Maybe is fatal only if you et it hover too long or indefinitely. Therefore, the way to leal with a long-playing Maybe is to shorten its duration: Give it a specific due date. For example, you could nudge t along with a response like, "You say, 'Maybe we can work something out in a few months.' Good. That gives is both time to think through my proposal. Do you agree hat a month and a half would be a reasonable length of ime in which to arrive at a decision? Then let's make an ppointment now to meet in a month and a half to reolve the situation." The Maybe is still there, but it's no onger a treacherous mire because it's been assigned a easible deadline.

You can even strengthen your chances of changing Maybe to Yes in a case like this. "You were saying how John likes to be involved in these situations. Do you think it would be a good idea for me to talk to John before I come back in a month and a half? Then the three of us can sit down and come to a decision." Now you've not only shortened the Maybe time-span, you've added an element to it that makes it more likely you'll be moving toward a Yes.

Just clarifying whether an answer really means Yes, No, or Maybe has helped me save an enormous amount of time. It also saves a lot of anxiety because I think there's nothing that produces more anxiety, in my business of fund-raising anyway, than hearing a Maybe.

The other Maybe is the one you get from somebody who, like all of us, hates to say No and to whom Maybe is the easy way out. The thinking is, "Maybe if I say Maybe rather than No, this person won't dislike me." (Even equivocators like to be liked.)

Maybe is also the answer you get from the quavering buyer who's afraid to make decisions. The propitiating or indecisive Maybe-maker needs your help, so you can both climb out of eternal limbo and reach a conclusion. When he or she mutters something vague such as, "Maybe, I'll think about it"—leaving you not knowing if you'll make the sale or should go and look elsewhere—your most useful response is an inquiry along the lines of, "What other options are you considering? Do you have someone else in mind to fill your need?" Or, "Obviously, you're interested in what I can do for you or you wouldn't be considering what I've said at all. Perhaps I can help you in making the decision. Tell me, will our size range work well for you? Do your stores need more junior sizes than you've been displaying?" The answer will give you the information you need to eventually reshape the inconclusive Maybe to a final Yes or No, and free you to go on from there.

Help for the Undecided

Many people really have a hard time making decisions. It's your job to help them. One technique you can use is write down the pros and cons of the situation as you ılk, so the other person can visualize the advantages and isadvantages. Build up the list of all the advantages first, riting them down one by one as you stress the positive, ıd then address yourself to the negatives. For example, ɔu're a sales representative for a dress company. The uyer, your prospect, is having trouble making a concrete ecision. You say, "I can hear that you are having trouble aking up your mind. Let's evaluate the line in terms of our needs. We'll check off each factor. From what ou've said, you find the line innovative, is that right?" Of course it's right; what you're doing is beginning to get ne agreement you'll try for all the way through your eeting.) "The styling is fresh; let's put that on our list. t's young; do you agree with that? And it's the right rice. Good! There seems to be something still holding ou back, though. Is it the size range? I know you special-ze in small sizes and it's true that this line doesn't come in ours; is that the problem? No? Then we'll write 'size ange' in the Advantage column. You say your problem is ou had trouble with my company's deliveries last year; ve promised you three weeks and you think you wound p last on the list. I can see how you feel; deliveries are a rucial problem."

Now you've succeeded in exposing the problem and an go ahead and figure out how to do something about t, without making idle promises. "I'm going to have a ses-ion with Sidney, who's in charge of traffic at our plant, o see about solving your problem by establishing priority hipments for you. Are we in agreement that if I call you ack this afternoon and guarantee that your orders will eceive priority attention, you'll be willing to participate n the fall line? Good! I'll have the contract on your desk y five o'clock."

Activating a Firm Answer

Another technique for moving the prospect who's interested in what you are selling but can't make a decision is to move him into an answer by giving him a reason to act. It's the scare technique, really, using phrases like "This may be too premature for your company" that imply you'll go to the competition with your innovative concept and he or she will miss the boat.

Then try to close the sale, or at least move closer to clarifying each of your positions.

You: I want to be fair with you about this because you look as if you are interested in what I'm describing. Is that true?

Prospect: Well, yes. I just don't know if what you propose is right for us at this time. I'd have to talk with some other people around here.

You: That's fair. Why don't you talk to them and meanwhile I'll set it up so you can have an exclusive on our product. Would you say three days would give you enough time to talk to your people?

Prospect: Good heavens, no. This is a huge organization and I have to clear it with a lot of people.

You: All right. What would be the time frame you would need?

Prospect: I could get the answer in two weeks.

You: Fine. I'll phone you then, in two weeks, to get your answer. If it's No, that's all right too. I just have to know the answer.

Sometimes you're faced with an undecided prospect, and a bureaucracy to plough through, too. It's not dificult to deal with if you understand how to shape your prospect's behavior. Watch this episode:

You: I can see that you're interested in having your junior executives attend our management training conference in October, and what's holding up your decision is all the department heads who have to OK the project. I'm just afraid that there are going to be a lot of other companies who'll want their people to attend the same conference, and you'll lose out. What I'll do is pencil in the reservations for you now, and if anybody else asks for those dates I'll call and let you know about it.

You've done two things here. You've motivated your prospect into walking the project through the bureaucracy for you. And you've presented the conference in such a way that he can see it as something real that is going to happen.

Now you can go on and extend the reality of your presentation to activate the decision-making: "If we set this conference up for you, how many people will attend? Our audio-visual room seats thirty people, and I can reserve all thirty spaces for you if you wish, or as many as you'll need. There's a special training film that suits your industry particularly well. I'll see if I can order it right away because I'm sure it'll mean a successful conference for you." Now your prospect has solid ammunition and will press for the OK's needed to give you the order. His or her Maybe will soon become a firm Yes or No.

The Well-Rounded Yes, No, or Maybe: Completing the Cycle

The reason Maybe is so tough is its nowhereness. It leaves you dangling, unable to complete the cycle you've begun. It's the undropped shoe, the endless song, the joke with no punchline. The incomplete cycle can drive you to lunacy. I know that what completely shatters me is when I'm talking to my husband and he doesn't respond. I can't focus on anything else that's going on until I'm acknowledged, assured that I've been heard and understood. You've had experiences of your own. Perhaps you've arranged to meet a friend at a restaurant so that you can talk over a certain problem. You sit down, give the waitress your orders, and she doesn't write, nod, or repeat what you've said. The cycle is not complete, and you and your friend can't get the conversation off the ground. You're dwelling only on whether your soups and salads are on the way.

That's what a Maybe does to you. Yes or No supplies completion; a Maybe is the undropped shoe. If you think about it for a moment, you can see how the completion of cycles comes up over and over in selling, just as it does in life, and how important it is to write *finis* on a project. When you sell a product or service, get a job or a raise, reach somebody by phone or get the appointment you've been shooting for, you've completed a cycle. Left incomplete, it's like a game that's unfinished: There can be no winner, ever.

7

How to Meet the People You Want to See: the rule of three

I haven't a clue in the world as to how to get started in a career. I mean, I don't know a soul in the business world I could offer my services to. Sure, I entertain a lot and have a lot of business people in my home. But so what? I was taught that it isn't nice to ask guests for anything for yourself. Anyway, why should they want to help *me*?

You have a product or service to sell, and you don't know the right people to sell it to. You would prefer not to call on anybody cold, and you figure that because Mr. or Ms. Prospective Buyer is not sitting on the end of your nose, you'll never get to meet him or her. But think for a moment. How do you suppose other salespeople get their contacts? Very simply, they use the contacts they already have to develop new ones.

Let me ask you a question:

Carole: Who would you like to meet next week?
You: Robert Redford.
Carole: OK. I don't know him, but I know somebody who's a friend of his agent. I'll speak to my contact and have him put you in touch with Redford's agent. The agent will put you in touch with Redford directly if you have something that's going to benefit his client.

What was just demonstrated is that you can get to anybody you want to, by the Rule of Three. One person always leads to another, who leads to a third. It's a human chain. And, by the Rule of Three, every person you know in the human chain is worth ten people. Here's how it works. The first person you talk to can steer you to three good contacts. Each of those three will lead to three more contacts of their own. Add it up: Three people times three contacts each, plus your original contact, equals ten valuable people.

The Importance of the Rule of Three

The importance of contacts and the Rule of Three cannot be overestimated. It's a rule successful people use every day of their selling lives. As a matter of fact, it's something you've been using all your nonselling life, too. Remember how you found your dressmaker? You asked a friend who she used for alterations, and she gave you her dressmaker's name and phone number. Or else she asked a friend of hers for the name of a good dressmaker. You got to the person you wanted by using a contact, and you didn't feel you were being rude or aggressive by asking. It's no different in selling. One person leads to another, and nearly everybody enjoys the feeling of helping someone else.

Advertising for Leads

In selling, you'll use contacts constantly. Say your goal is to find a job as a dental hygienist. The best way to advertise your need is to talk about it. Get the word out. Discuss your goal with everybody you meet who could conceivably lead you to a dentist who needs a hygienist. The more you put out the word, the more chances there are that somebody instrumental will hear what your goal is, and the more readily you will move toward it.

Contacts as a Calling Card

Contacts also provide the identification and credentials that open doors to people who never heard of you. Successful people use them all the time. When you have to make a cold call, the first thing to do is name-drop, make a connection through a mutual contact. Telephone and say something like, "I was talking with Jack Fastfood the other day and he suggested I call you to make an appointment. He thought you'd be interested in a project my company's been working on." Introducing yourself by attaching a name to what you're asking for invariably takes the "cold" out of cold calls. It's an unwritten law of business life that no matter how harried an executive is, if somebody calls and a friend or colleague's name is attached, you give that person extra attention.

Keep Track of Your Contacts

Good contacts have tonnage, and as a good salesperson you should collect them for when you need weight to throw around. A very efficient method is to record every potential contact's name and connections on a three-by-five-inch file card. The cards should contain the crucial information that memory is likely to lose: name, address, phone number, business affiliation, where and when you met, the circumstances and conversation, specific people and things that were mentioned.

Reality: *You can meet anybody in this world you need to meet by using the Rule of Three.*

The People You'll See on Appointments

In order to make an appointment to sell, you have to have somebody to sell to. Therein may lie a catch: The somebodys who are your sellees may not always be the people you'd choose as friends. The reality of that is, irrational beliefs and prejudices about who you ought to mingle with or sell to can get in the way of reaching your goal.

Again and again I meet perfectly capable women who live on leftovers from childhood, still taking on faith what their elders taught: "Nice girls mix only with nice people." Rubbish. I tell these women, "Get rid of your little-girl emotional baggage. Trade it in for logical reality: The reason you sell to someone is because selling is your goal, not because the person is cultured and genteel."

My friend Barbara gave me a simile that illuminates the matter of who you're willing to sell to. She was giving her son a birthday party and asked who he'd like to invite. David reeled off a list of friends, but omitted the name of one boy with whom he played baseball every day. Puzzled, his mother asked why. David explained that the reason he played with the boy every day was because he was a good pitcher, not somebody he'd like to invite to his party. At age ten, David already understood that it is not only all right, but also desirable to deal with somebody professionally with whom you'd have nothing to do personally. Being "nice" has nothing to do with having a good pitching arm.

Then there was the man who came to address one of my workshops and inadvertently taught us a lesson on "who you're willing to sell to." He was an archetypical male chauvinist: vain, opinionated, arrogant in his sexism. Called us "the girls" and all that. After the class one student cornered me, irate and sputtering. She wished I'd never asked the man to speak, he'd spoiled everything for her, she would never ever sell to a person like that. We sat down and I asked her the eye-opener question: "Then who *would* you sell to?" I asked her if she thought all her customers had to look like her, have her values, her style, dress like her, use her language. When I told her *my* customer criterion—I sell only to people who pay their bills—she got the point.

People Worth Selling To

There's a way of spotting who is and who isn't worth selling to. When you find a person or company whose attitude is to survive, forget them. You're not going to get paid, in cash or anything else, because a survivor is one who's hanging on by the fingernails, grasping at whatever or whoever might keep him/her minimally alive. Survivors are at the bottom of the sell-to ladder.

Perched one rung above is the company or person whose dominant theme is security. They watch their money and their positions very carefully. Need all kinds of proof that you are the right person or have the right product or service. They need to get their security from other people. You can do business with them, but with caution. They'll try to whittle you down: "I can't quite afford that, but if you'll do it for two thousand dollars less . . ." Either get yourself a tightly written contract or forget the security-ridden prospect. You need a guarantee, with that type, that you're not wasting your time and talent.

At the top of the ladder is the best type of all, the "social" company or individual. They're characterized by being open, willing to spread out. They're generous, share creative thoughts, develop ideas along with you, are joyous when you both benefit. "Social" is a winner: a proven, actualized, self-confident, and cooperative person or company who's fun and rewarding to work with.

The Characters You'll Meet

There are myriad types of people you'll meet as sellees. Some of them wear double-knits and white socks with black shoes, but underneath the double-knit may be somebody who is worth your selling time. Or perhaps not; you have to assess the value of the time the person will require and make your decision accordingly.

The Whirlwind. This is the very busy person who never has time, whose thoughts are never in sequence, whose actions have nothing to do with the discussion. The real problem is he or she is so disorganized he/she can't keep appointments, make commitments, or be logical. He or she will consume your time as if it were the Last Supper. But if he or she is a real opportunity, the only person who can make the buy, you'll just have to put up with the Whirlwind. An acquaintance who's a TV news director is in that position. He really has only three places where he can sell himself: ABC, CBS, and NBC. So he has no choice but to stick with those outlets, even though it's torture to pin down the people he must meet with.

The Placater. This is the nicest person you ever want to meet. Says everything he/she thinks you want to hear, short of a definite Yes or No. He or she is too scared of rocking the boat to make any decisions. Your job is to move him/her out of Maybe. An effective way to do that is to make him or her your passport to the person who does have the power to buy. Take the Placater along with you as you move up to where the power is. Enlist his/her aid and make him or her look good in the process. Let's assume you're selling travel packages for executives and the Placater has been ever so nice, but won't make a commitment to buy. "We'll see. It sounds lovely, but we'll see." Now's the time to suggest a three-way meeting with John Buyingpower, where you can back up the Placater in presenting the package you want to sell and wind up with a three-way win.

The Competitor. This one's no fun. Has to win, no matter what. Always has to be right, tops you all over the place. If you cite an example of a successful travel package you've put together for another company, he'll tell you about the one *he* invented that's even better. You say the cost of a group charter to Las Vegas is $800 per person; he knows for a fact it costs $810. You can't beat the Competitor at his own game and it doesn't pay to try. The prime rule of selling is never ever to make anybody wrong, and with the Competitor, if you're right that means he's wrong. So help him be right, since that's what he so desperately needs. It's what you'd do anyway if you were selling to somebody who didn't have to keep displaying how terrific he is. Whether it's worth your time and irritation depends on the Competitor's value to you as a purchaser.

The Blamer. Whatever you say, you're going to be blamed for something. Things are always somebody else's fault, with the Blamer. "Nellie in bookkeeping hasn't done her job right, so I can't give you a budget for what you propose." That's the Blamer's way of not taking responsibility for making a decision. Nothing can get done because somebody else hasn't done his or her job. The Blamer requires a lot of manipulation if you want to win a sale.

The Leveler. My ideal, the White Knight with all the right attributes. He or she is on the rise, fast. Influential, intelligent, reasonable, amiable. Knows who he/she is, where he/she is going, and how best to get there. Will help you as readily as you help him/her because he or she is as eager as you are to further a career. The Leveler is the best sellee of the lot, a mover who's willing to make decisions, take realistic risks, be wide open to whatever you can provide that will move him/her ahead even faster. He/she will make good things happen for you because you will benefit him or her.

8

The Art of Making Dates

I think the thing that bothers me most is setting up an appointment, because I find that even with the tools I have for getting through the secretary, once I've gotten through to the person I want to talk to, he'll still resist me. He'll try to weasel out of making a date, or even make one and then cancel it. What I do is keep calling and calling. It may take weeks or months to set up an appointment, but once I get there, everything is OK. I'm sure it's just the telephone situation people resist.

They never call you back. They're always in meetings or out to lunch. I leave my number once, twice, and then I'm embarrassed to keep pestering.

Make no mistake, getting an appointment to meet with your prospect is a giant and often difficult step. Miss it and you can forget all the rest. It's easy to miss, too. Executives are harried people and their schedules don't pernit making priorities of new business such as yours. What ou have to do is make seeing you a priority.

Defrosting the Cold Call

> I shuffle my contact cards around on my desk all day long, hating to pick up the phone and make the calls. Hating to chance getting a No. But I know that if I don't pick up the phone, I'll never get the appointments I must have. It's a circular agony for me.

One of the toughest of all appointments to get is when you're calling cold. It's the same as a blind date: Neither party really wants any part of it. The social caller has to find some way to break the ice and gain acceptance, usually by mentioning a mutual friend's name, a common interest, or a strong competitive edge. The same applies to a cold call in business. If you're an unknown and you want an appointment, you'd best find a way to make yourself desirable.

The call-warmer of choice is the use of a contact. "I was speaking with your friend Connie last week and she suggested I contact you about an idea I have that she believes would benefit your company." The "idea" could be in the product you sell, the service you have to offer, the employment or assignment you want.

One of the hardest transitions to make is when you've worked for a large corporation and no longer have that credential. Being able to say, "This is Susan Brown of the Mammoth Corporation" carries a lot of weight. "This is Susan Brown" conveys little. You need the connection, so it's, "My friend Max tells me that he saw you at your club last week and you mentioned that you're looking for an expert fashion photographer. I've worked for *Vogue, Mademoiselle,* and . . ."

Anne-Marie, a relocation expert, frequently has to make cold calls. She says that for her they're the most horrid part of the whole selling routine. Listen:

> The worst part of the selling process is the initial telephone contact. I think it's especially difficult for me because in my case the people I need to make appointments with are personnel managers. Try convincing a switchboard operator that you're not looking for a job when you ask for the name of the personnel manager. He or she invariably snaps, "We don't have any jobs. Just send in your résumé." I have to keep explaining that I'm not looking for a job, that I have something to offer that the personnel manager will be interested in. Most times I have to call back a half-dozen times, until I get a different operator who will put me through.

An insurance consultant describes her experiences with cold calls this way:

> Sometimes I send a personal letter and follow it by a phone call, sometimes I do it the other way around. Either way, the letter is really a backup for the call. Once in a while, I do a buckshot mailing and send out a letter to maybe 150 prospects. Even though I only expect one or two percent response, the letter is there and I can use it as a reason for calling. Other times, when I've just barely met somebody and no real contact has been established, I'll break the ice for my phone call with a letter such as this:
>
> > Dear Ms. Jones:
> >
> > That was indeed an inspiring evening at the Insurance Women's Club. I strongly believe that if Rotary Club dinner meetings work for men, they should work for us, too.

For the past fourteen years I have headed the Executive Businesswoman's Division of ABC Insurance Company. We have been very successful in catering to the needs of women interested in protecting themselves and their families against loss of income. You may know some of our clients; they include Margo White, Susan Brown, Emma Green, and Betsy Black—all of whom, like you, are heads of advertising agencies.

Because I am interested in expanding our client roster, I am taking the liberty of attaching a brief questionnaire in the hope that either you or someone in your firm might want more information about ABC. I am interested in doing business with women whenever possible, and hope you share this attitude.

Enclosed please find a brief description of our service, the questionnaire, and a stamped return envelope. Many thanks, in advance, for your kindness and I hope to see you again in the near future.

Cordially,

What to Do with the Cold Response

Often when you're asking for an appointment you'll find yourself on the receiving end of a chilly response such as, "We're not interested." Or, "We already have your kind of service." Or, "We don't have a budget for your service." A follow-up letter can change that implied "No" to a "Yes, come in and see us" if it contains a hand-tailored benefit for the prospect. You can arrive at what will intrigue him or her by finding out, either through prior research or on the phone, what the company already *has* by way of your kind of service. With this information, you can then offer them what they *lack.* If it's a case of "We already have some," you can state a way that you can supplement the existing service. If it's "We have no money" and your research says that they do spend but that this fiscal year is taken, you can plant seeds for the future: "I understand that you have budget limitations for this fiscal quarter. I feel, nonetheless, that it would be worth our meeting to explore the possibilities for your next fiscal year."

Getting Past the Secretary

Sometimes the cold call doesn't get off the ground simply because you can't get past a secretary. Before you put all the blame on her or him, though, listen to what Edna has to say:

> I've been his secretary for twenty years. I sure know how this place works, and I'd be happy to help the salespeople get appointments with the right people—if they wouldn't be so uptight. Some of them hear a woman's voice on the other end, and I know they're saying "dumb secretary." "I want to talk to the boss," they say to me. They see my boss listed in the book as head of the department and decide they'll only talk to him. He *is* the head of the department, but he doesn't make the buying decision. His deputies do that, and I know just which ones are interested in what. Some of the women who call are the worst. They spend weeks calling, always missing their prospect because he's in meetings. I know they're trying to sell something and are calling from long distances to set up a meeting. But they make believe it's "a personal matter." Or they say, "I'd rather talk to him directly." And I figure if they don't think enough of me to at least inform me, then I'll just take the message and let it go at that. I could really do

them some good, too. But if they keep insisting that the person with the title is the only one who will help them, I just can't worry about them. There was a woman last year who really enlisted my help. She was calling from California and told me all about her product. It was fascinating but unusual. I didn't think anyone in our department would be interested, but I asked around. I asked one of the librarians who the right person would be for this product, and she came up with someone. Next time this saleswoman called, I had a name for her, and I helped her make the appointment. She made her sale, and she sent me a lovely plant for my desk—she really didn't have to—and I felt really good that it had worked out so well. As I said, it really does feel good to help other people get where they want to go.

The Secretary: Friend or Foe

What you get when you phone somebody for an appointment is the secretary, the guardian. There are those who are like the secretary whose feelings you just read about, and there is the type who plays office wife and views you as a threat simply because you're another woman. You are somebody to be kept away from her employer and out of her daytime marriage. And while her fantasy is unreal, she is real and you are going to have to deal with her. In fact, you are going to have to deal with both types.

The best way to do this is to incorporate the guardian into your process. Make her your ally. Ask her name when you give yours. Become her friend so that she becomes a person for you and you become a person to her. Get her involved with what you are doing by telling her about your product or service and how it has helped people like her boss. "We have helped people like your boss makes lots of money, save money, publicize their name." You give her a benefit, so you'll have a spokesperson on your side saying, "Hey, this woman sounds interesting. She has a way to really help you and besides, she's a personal friend of Connie Contact." You can get information, as well, to assist you in winning your sale. Ask what her employer does, exactly; what needs her company has; what she'd like to see happening in the firm.

If she's really a dragon lady and you can't get through, make your phone calls at 8 A.M. or after 5 when she probably won't be there and the person you're trying to reach will have to pick up the telephone personally.

Another way to get through to the person you want an appointment with is to telephone or write to the secretary in the same way you would approach her employer. "Mark Jones and I were discussing your company a few evenings ago, and he suggested that I see your employer, Mr. Smith, because he felt that my work would be of particular interest to your company. I'll be in your neighborhood on Wednesday and Thursday, the thirtieth and thirty-first, and I would like to make an appointment on one of those two days at Mr. Smith's convenience." Incidentally, putting the contact's name first, "Mark Jones and I," is a subtlety that adds weight, both by putting your credential up front and by introducing yourself via a name that is already familiar.

Or you can arouse the guardian's empathy: "I can't seem to get through to meet with your boss. Is he not interested in me? Or is he not interested in this kind of widget? What's the best way of getting to see him? What would *you* suggest we do?" "We." You're in this together now. You're making her feel that her help is important and that she is important. Telling her, "I know I can rely n you to get that information through. You're the only ne who can really help me," lets her know that you recgnize her power and invites her to exhibit it to you by ollowing through.

Lillian, a securities analyst, has learned important essons in fielding difficult secretaries' ploys and, as a reult, has succeeded in winning sales that once were lost to er. She reports, "After a year at this, I've become quite uccessful at selling. One thing that's helped immensely is aving learned how often a secretary will try power plays. he'll say, 'I'm sorry, so-and-so is busy' or 'I can't get hrough to him.' I didn't know how to deal with that at irst, and I wasted a lot of time just getting put off by ecretaries. Now I play their games and try to make myelf sound as important as possible so that I'll get through o the person I want. Very often, if I'm trying to make an ppointment with someone and the secretary says, 'Sond-so is busy,' I'll say, 'This is the Giant Corporation alling.' Or if she says, 'So-and-so is busy and can't talk to ou right now, I'll say, 'He asked me to call and give him ertain information.' I'll even lie if I have to, to get hrough to that person. I wouldn't have done that in the eginning. One just has to be more assertive. Also, I hink women don't take themselves seriously if they're ust starting. They think, 'Well, it's not the real thing.' You have to come to the place where you say, 'This is erious. This is a job. This is the work world and if I want o succeed I've got to play it the way it works.'"

Reality: *Selling is persistence.*

One of the greatest astonishments to the novice in selling is the exasperating number of times you may have to telephone before you actually get your prospect on the line. It can take the persistence and patience of Alexander Graham Bell himself to get through, to get that "one win out of ten" that counts. A friend of mine who's a book designer recently moved east from courtly New Mexico and ran up against the most frustrating experiences of her career, trying to break into the frantically paced New York market. She says, "People just don't return phone calls here. I couldn't believe it at first, but they don't. I'd keep leaving my name and number, and I'd never hear back. I'd call the same person once, twice a week for weeks and the signal was always 'He's busy. He's out. He's in conference. Call back in a week.' It was so daunting.

"Now I've learned how to handle it. I *do* keep calling back umpteen times until I get through, and I do *not* let myself feel put down or insulted. I realize that I'm just one of hundreds of people trying to reach the same busy executive. Out of all those pink 'While You Were Out' slips piled up on his desk, the only calls he'll have time to return are the ones that look important. So, I just call as many times as it takes for him to get the cue that my call is important."

The attitude, "I called him, now it's his turn to call me" gets you nothing but long fruitless waits. The dripping faucet routine gets you action. Keep calling and you'll get more appointments. Get more appointments and you'll get more sales. It's simply a matter of statistics again.

Reality: *If you can't make an appointment you can't make a sale. The art of making appointments is a basic in the art of selling.*

"I Could Scream Every Time I *Look* at a Phone"

f telephoning is hard for you, write yourself a script in advance, so you'll know what you want to say, and say it. You can lose track and control by winging phone conversations. Rehearse your script, too, so you'll hear how it sounds and be comfortable with it when you're actually on the phone. "Good morning, Mr. Smith. John Jones suggested I call to make an appointment with you. He feels that my style of work as a professional fashion photographer is exactly what you're looking for right now."

Plan the time you'll be on the phone for only a minute or two. In New York that's all you're going to get. In smaller towns and other parts of the country, the pace is more leisurely and you'll be encouraged to insert pleasantries and asides. Go right ahead and make the most of the getting-to-know-you opportunity, but keep in mind that your goal is to get an appointment because you have something beneficial to offer. You want a Yes to your request, or at least a No. Never let your prospect ramble off with a Maybe. Make sure the cycle's completed.

If you have so large a number of phone calls to make that the very idea is daunting, slice the number into segments: eight on Monday, eight on Tuesday, and so on until the list is completed and you've reached your goal. Completing that telephone cycle will permit you to go on to the next set of goals on your agenda. And if it happens that Tuesday is a poor day for you, don't worry about making the eight calls that day. Just crank them into other days; what's important is that you meet your end deadline.

Two more bits of advice. If you've already explored

and have the information you need, use or consider hiring an assistant to make the appointments for you. Having somebody whose time is less valuable than yours do the phoning saves you time, money, and the annoyance of having to do groundwork you don't savor.

My second bit of advice is this: Telephone with a positive attitude, and the response you get will more likely be positive, too. Always assume that the person you are calling has been waiting to hear the benefit you're about to offer.

Your Prospect's on the Phone. What Do You Say to Make Him/Her See You?

You get his attention and arouse his interest and desire fast. If you have a contact, always lead with it: "Mr./Ms. Jones, Connie Contact suggested I call you . . ." Or, lacking the contact, find another connection: "I saw an item in the *Wall Street Journal* about the problem you're having currently with your lawsuit and I have some information I believe would help you. I'd like to come see you this Wednesday or Thursday to discuss it. Which day would be better for you?" Use this approach *only* if you are very sure of your facts, when you have an inside line and know what you have is what they're looking for. Otherwise, you're going to waste your time and infuriate your would-be customer.

What you're doing is putting your benefit up front, without giving it all away, and then limiting his or her choices to *when,* not *if* he or she will see you. "I'll be in your neighborhood Wednesday and Thursday. Which is better for you?—You can't make it this week? How about next week: Monday or Tuesday?"

When Not to Make an Appointment

But before you say Monday or Tuesday, find out if it's going to be worth your while and what you should bring with you by asking questions. If your exploration reveals that you've nothing to win by making an appointment, don't. As a magazine space saleswoman puts it, "I never force an appointment until I know what the budget is."

When you get the date you want, I'm sure you're aware that your tone of voice will have had something to do with it. Enthusiasm and sincerity come through as unmistakably and contagiously by phone as they do in person. The difference is, on the phone you don't have the confirming underscore of facial expression or body language. That's why successful people consciously practice projecting a good telephone voice.

9

Selling When the Product is You

> When I'm selling myself, I'm always anxious because I always have to make sure I'm making a positive self-presentation. In essence, what I'm selling is trust. I'm also selling the information and skills that I have to give, but I'm really selling trust. It causes me a lot of anxiety because I'm really on the line and very vulnerable.

Today, tomorrow, any number of times in your career you're going to face the awesome mission of getting yourself a job, a raise, a promotion, or an increase in rates for what you do. If you're normal, you'll black out. "This isn't selling," you'll say. "This is different. It's me—taking a step *toward* selling. First I get the job or promotion, then I have something to sell."

Right, and wrong. Yes, it *is* you. No, it's the same; you're selling from first to last. Because selling is how you will get a job or raise, a promotion or fee increase. You'll use exactly the same attitude and abilities as when you deal with a product or service. In both circumstances, what you are doing is persuading, convincing, influencing, manipulating people into wanting to buy what you have. The only difference, if it helps you to look at it as a difference, is that when no product is involved what you are persuading people to buy is your ability to fill a need. Your ability is the product. In other words, the product is you. And selling yourself—your ability to fill a need—demands skills and knowledge identical to selling land, or food, or nuts and bolts.

Reality: *Selling is selling, whether it's yourself or a product.*

What Do You Want and Why Do You Want It?

Step one, as always, is to step back and examine the realities. What are you shooting for, exactly, and is it a reasonable target for you at this point? Is the change one you can afford? How will the job, raise, or promotion advance your career and move you toward your long-range goals? Have you put a timetable on completing your objective? Now is the time, at the outset, to make sure you're not hacking away haphazardly at an undertaking that may not be appropriate or desirable for you; to dissect the issues one by one and formulate concrete conclusions.

A situation analysis is definitely called for.

- Where are you now in your career?
- Where can it lead if you stay there?
- What's in it for you if you switch?

- What do you want that necessitates change? Why or how will change be an improvement?

Think in Specifics

Say you've been a junior loan officer at a bank for three years and you believe a promotion to head loan officer is what you want now. Why? Because it seems a natural progression? Your friends will think more of you? It means more money? You're aiming at the bank manager's job?

Be clear on your real motivation. Is banking what you want to stay with, or have you a stronger affinity? Should you use your bank to get experience in accounting rather than loans?

If another field beckons, is this the right time to move into it? Have you accrued enough knowledge and accreditation to move on? Is the grass really greener over there or will the economics, the opportunities, the corporate game be a no-woman's-land for you?

Don't Make A Move Until You Research It

If you want to stay out of trouble, avert mistakes, and be effective in whatever you do professionally or personally, assume nothing. Ever. When the car in front of you speeds up, don't assume the light has turned green. Take a moment and check it out for yourself. When you find the perfect apartment, don't assume utilities are included in the rent. Ask about all the costs in detail. Just so, when you decide you want a job, a raise, a promotion, or an increase in your rates, dig in and get all the facts before you barge ahead.

I repeat in loud caps: ASSUME NOTHING. EVER.

Research the Terrain

One of the first things you'll want to find out for sure is what possibilities are open to you in your field of interest. You'll need to learn everything you can about the market, the competition, the industry as a whole, and the product or service in particular. Ascertain who makes and influences the decision to buy what you have to offer. Find out who your competition is, what qualifications you need, what your prospect is looking for. Learn the field and the company: What is the target market, what are the objectives, the goals, what is your prospect's competitive advantage and how can yours fit in with it. Explore what the general trends are and how you can help your prospect lead the competition. If certain tools such as writing a proposal or a contract are necessary and they're foreign to you, ask somebody to show you how to do it. Never be afraid to ask questions, even when you're being interviewed. Your interest and intelligence will be noted and appreciated. Nobody expects you to be Wonder Woman with all the answers, and you can err disastrously by making assumptions, trying to guess rather than being up-front.

Research means talking to friends, colleagues, anybody in or out of the business whom you can buttonhole to supply information. It means attending organization dinners and seminars, to keep abreast of what's going on, to make contacts, to learn what other successful people have done. It means keeping up on what's what and who's who through business publications, books, brochures, company reports—every relevant piece of literature you can get your hands on. It's listening for buzzwords and ideas, picking up information about corporate philosophy and self-image, exploring the firm's and the field's current financial picture and its plans or potential for expansion.

You Never Outgrow Your Need for Research

Whatever stage you're at, whether you are on the climb or an old pro, you need to stay on top of the ever-changing scene. The way to do it is to be active in trade associations, at least two of them, for information and contacts. Subscribe to the journals and newsletters in your trade or profession, to keep up on new developments and concepts. Cultivate at least four good sources for gossip, to be in the know: who's been fired, what new business is breaking, where things are opening up. Lunch out often, throw cocktail parties, make a point of swapping shop-talk. Get in on the gossip network and you're in on the latest news in town.

Ongoing research applies at all levels. Jane is the president of a thriving company, and she's interested in the possibility of getting into direct mail. In order to be armed with inside information based on experience, she's set a research schedule for herself: six meetings a month for three months with people who are involved in some aspect of direct mail. The first month she took three research sources to lunch, invited one to her home for dinner, and conferred by phone with two more. At the end of ninety days, Jane will assemble the information gleaned from her eighteen interviews and sit down with her key staff to determine what course to pursue during the next three-month period.

The Case of a Successful Researcher

Anne-Marie is a French-born woman who specializes in relocating people whose companies—her clients—regularly transfer executives and their families from other countries to Atlanta. Her services provide a means of easing the transition by helping to locate appropriate housing, schools, transportation, physicians, cultural amenities, and so on.

Anne-Marie went into business for herself three years ago, but not until she'd done thorough preliminary research to find out whether it was a profitable idea or not. She checked out other relocation companies in Atlanta, talking with them and their clients, read trade publications, got government statistics and information from every available source. She learned how many competitors she would have; what she could offer that they could not; how many prospects she could realistically turn into clients; and what her fees should be, based on overhead and the going rates.

Before Anne-Marie could go out and sell her services she needed to find the clients who could buy them. So her next "locating" job was for herself: She researched the marketplace for likely prospects. In her words, here is exactly how she went about it.

> How do I find the companies who need my services? I know that they have to be international; I have staked my competitive advantage on the fact that I am multilingual. I know that they have to be major corporations, with the money to spend on personnel transfers. And I know that they have to have an office in Atlanta, where I operate. So I start with the Fortune 500 and 100 lists. I look to see which companies have offices in Atlanta as well as in other countries. If I don't use the Fortune list, I use

one of the other specialized directories; there's one for every field at the library.

I may not always be in business for myself. I think I may want to work for another company someday. I know just how I'll go about finding who would need me most. What I'll do is look up which relocation companies have offices in Atlanta. In my case, I'll concentrate on those with an international clientele because of my advantage in being multilingual. I'll research personally and through contacts whenever possible to learn what it is these companies need, what they lack. I'll try to find out what their self-image is, so I won't make the mistake of threatening them by saying, 'I'm going to take over and change the way you do things.' I'll find out everything I can in advance, to learn how I could fit into the organization.

Another way to do research on your prospects, especially if you're looking for a job, is to have exploratory interviews with minor companies in your field of interest. Never the key ones; you save those for the sell. I'd want to learn what people in relocation need, and I'd want to pick up whatever contacts I could, too. A good approach, I've found, is not to apply for a job but to call on another matter. For example, I take a lot of continuing education courses and I could assign myself a paper to explore the industry. Or, since I like to write, I could find a publication that needs a story and ask somebody for an interview. Or I could teach a course and invite people who interest me to be guest speakers. People are very generous about sharing their experiences and feelings and knowledge. It makes *them* feel good, at the same time it gives others great understanding of business or professions.

Do Research On Yourself, As Well

Know who your competition is. What salary you'll need, to cover your costs and make a profit. List your strengths nd see how they can be used as benefits in the field or rm you want to enter. Establish whether you are realis-ically in line for a certain job, or if promotion is always rom within. Would the job be a good training ground or your own further advancement? Would the raise ou're asking for be in line with comparable jobs in the ame or other firms or fields?

Arm yourself to the teeth with all the statistics you an unearth.

Reality: *Homework in depth always pays off.*

Be Hardheaded

Are you committed enough to put a deadline on your nove and stick to it? Have you a written-down schedule, goal timetable? Putting off job-hunts and interviews is he most alluring of all traps. Rationalizing, "One of these lays I'll really do something about it," is much easier than getting out there and hustling. Or wrestling the enemy, ear of rejection. Are you willing to follow through and get what you want—really?

Pay Your Dues

Finally, are you willing to give up something as well as to gain? There's a trade-off for everything. That's some-thing you have to accept, going in. If you want a face-lift you must accept having tiny scars. If you want a job in Chicago, you'll have to abandon your house and friends in Peoria. If you want to sell your first song, TV script, novel, you'll have to give up your dream of a fifty-thousand dollar sale in exchange for creating a track record at a much lower fee. At Child Research Service, which has been an established business since 1966, we have to be willing to take on jobs we know we'll lose money on, as the trade-off for gaining accreditation in fields that are new to us.

Here is a story about trade-offs for validation th
may ring a bell for you. Marion had reached the poi
where she could leave off being a housewife and moth
and get out on her own. Never having worked, her ski
were limited. But there was one thing she liked and w
good at: cooking. So Marion decided she wanted to go
work for one of the gourmet-chef cooking schools in h
city. First she sent out résumés but, lacking profession
credentials, that effort netted nothing. So she lowere
her aim for her immediate goal and set about offerin
her services as an unpaid apprentice. She telephone
cooking school chef after chef, saying: "I'll sweep you
floors and scrub your pots and pans if you will give m
the opportunity to sit at your feet." Her offer hit hom
with one of the chefs and for four months Marion swe
floors, cleaned pots and pans, and observed the maestr
at work.

Then one day she found herself in the familia
leading-lady-breaks-a-leg situation. The chef became i
just before a demonstration and suddenly Marion was th
only suitable stand-in for the star. There she was, th
school's sole teacher of gourmet cooking. Naturally, sh
killed herself. Memorized Larousse. Mimicked ever
technique she'd seen the chef employ. Worked like a de
vish teaching soup, soufflé, and salad to the class. It wa
great experience and when the chef returned, Mario
approached him with, "Now I know that I am able t
teach cooking well, and no longer wish to be your helpe
I want my own class to instruct. I see you have you
doubts, so I will prove to you that I really have done
good job."

The proof was in letters of commendation Mario
asked her satisfied students to send to the chef. The
were her accreditation and with them, Marion got he

own class. The several months she had labored as Cinderella were her dues-paying trade-off for the validation that enabled her to get the job she really wanted.

Where to Find a Job

There are three basic sources for job-hunters: ads, employment services, and contacts. And the greatest of these is contacts.

Newspaper ads are probably the poorest. Most of the good jobs are taken quickly—by people who hear about them through the gossip-and-contact network, or they are filled from within. And when good jobs *are* advertised in the paper, there's a slew of competition for them. Not to say that a lot of good jobs aren't found by following the ads; they are. But a lot of good jobs are never advertised at all.

Employment agencies and executive searchers are fine, but they have their drawbacks, too. As middlemen and women, searchers may not always have the correct information, or they may screen you out because you don't fit into their written job descriptions. It's much easier for them to work with people who can be readily pigeonholed, people who are ready-made matchups with job specifications. If you're changing fields, a great deal of creative thought and work may have to go into categorizing you so you can be placed in a waiting pigeonhole.

Your best bet, when you're looking for a job or assignment, a raise or promotion, is to use contacts. Advertise your needs. Talk to people—with appropriate discretion, of course. If you are in a job, you want to keep the atmosphere happy until you actually move on. There are ways to get the word out without putting your head o the block. What you want is to have your contacts with ir fluence or information put you in touch with the righ people. And, if you remember the Rule of Three, eac person you mention your needs to will become a suppor system of ten people who can help you fill them.

Perhaps you know far in advance that you're goin to move on. Ethel had that experience: She told her em ployer a whole year in advance that she wanted to furthe her career by getting into an allied field. For that whol year she had the support, encouragement, and good con tacts of everyone in the office. It was an enormously help ful way to find the job that was right for her.

The contacts you reach out to can put you in touch with a potential employer, but usually cannot guarante that you'll get the job. That part's up to you, your re search, and how well you use it. An instance came u recently that I'd like to pass along to you because th follow-through was so imaginative.

A friend had called and asked me to see Ginny, a young woman he'd met at a trade show. Because of th contact, I made the appointment—I'll always make tim for somebody when there's a friend's name attached Ginny turned out to be personable but inexperienced and there was no trainee slot in my company where sh could be placed. However, she evidenced such enthusi asm and came forth with so many good ideas that I sai Yes to three more meetings. At each meeting she woul ask questions about the company and the industry. Ther she'd go out, do some research, and call me back with ideas and solutions. She was doing my work for me, and doing it well. She became so valuable that she created a position for herself. She'll be joining our firm in three months.

A young man told me how research paid off for him. Bob is a skilled language workshop leader and had the idea of selling his ability to a local university. He says, "I went out to the college to find out who needed workshops and discovered that I had a lot of competition in the language department; I'd be just one more person begging for a job if I stayed in that niche. So I dug in to find out the best way to present myself. I met with some thirty different people—professors, students, secretaries—and learned from my survey that the competition for jobs was among the salaried professors. What that meant to me was that I should approach the continuing education department, where they let you try anything if it'll attract student enrollment. I worked up a proposal for the department head and assured him that I knew from research that the community needed language workshops, and that I personally knew ten people who would enroll. I told him I was confident I could get together a system that would keep people coming in. I also set it up so he'd have nothing to lose. He was concerned about the cost of advertising the workshop, and I said, 'You don't have to advertise because I want to start the course in two weeks, so the advertising wouldn't make any difference.' It worked. I didn't come in asking for a job, I came in with an attractive plan that didn't cost the department anything. I got what I wanted and the workshops have been very successful."

The Invent-a-Niche Method

A fourth and superb source for getting a job or a promotion is to see or create a need, and then fill it. Here are a couple of situations based on events that really happened that will activate your imagination so you can devise programs of your own.

Assume you're a secretary at Survey & Analysis, Inc It's a young corporation and on the grow. So are you and what you want to build is a career, not just a job Your next goal is to move up within S & A, Inc., but a this stage in its growth the company must limit its person nel and there are no vacant slots you might fill. You create one. To begin, you study and analyze the organiza tion and its problems. As a secretary, you're in a position to see that the firm is in a tight financial position and tha one way to reduce overhead would be to investigate using alternate suppliers. On your own, you conduct the appro priate research and then present your findings to the president. You offer to effect continued savings in return for the heretofore nonexistent duties and salary of office manager.

Take another situation. For three years you have done a creditable job as account executive at an advertis- ing agency. You want to move up. So, through a contact you bring in a new client whose cosmetics business is one the agency's not dealt with before. You understand the cosmetics business, having researched the field, and fur- thermore the new client is personally cemented to you. You explain to the agency president the size of the new client's budget, its immediate profit and its potential, and how handling the account will attract additional clients from other areas of women's products. What you ask for in exchange for bringing in the valuable new client is the title and salary of account supervisor of the agency's beauty and fashion division—which you've just invented.

In both of these scenarios you have observed a need and then devised a means to fulfill it. You have gotten your promotion by selling a product: yourself, your abil- ity to fill a need. And if you think about it, you have called upon your life experience as a woman, transferring your ability to empathize with friends to your employer: "I realize what you need, I sympathize with your problem, and now I would like you to consider my solution."

Share a Job and Fill a Need

For many women who want to work, full-time employment is not practical or possible. They've children to tend, want to study for a degree, or have some other commitment they don't wish to break. But part time is not only hard to find, traditionally it's been more job- than career-oriented, therefore not fully satisfying. There's a new and growing movement that reverses the difficulties of building a career through part-time work, however, and it may be the solution for you. It's called job-sharing and to show you how it works, I'll tell you about a job-sharing team, Susan and Liz.

They were young mothers, and friends. They'd been hunting and hunting, each on her own, for part-time somethings that would allow them to work and take care of their homes and families, too. No luck. Then Liz heard about a particularly appealing job opening in career counseling, something they both were able to do and liked. She had a brilliant idea and after talking it over with Susan, the two presented their proposal to the guidance office that had the job opening. "We are here as a team," Liz said. "We are both skilled career counselors and we both want the job. However, we both have outside responsibilities that don't allow either of us to work full time. I am suggesting that you hire us both for the price of one. I'll come in mornings, while Susan takes care of my child at her home. In the afternoons Susan will take over the counseling job here, and I'll fill in for her at home. If one of us is ill or has an emergency, we're free to trade times between ourselves, and you won't have the problem of absenteeism. There's another advantage for you: If one of us doesn't hit it off with a student, the other can take on that case."

Susan and Liz got the job and their sharing arrangement has provided a benefit they didn't foresee. Exchanging enthusiasm and information about their job has generated increased self-confidence and expertise for both women.

Find a Need and Fill It: Diane's Story

Diane is more than a fashion designer; she is an entrepreneurial fashion designer. As she puts it, "I don't want to ride home in somebody else's wagon. I'm not content just to design clothes for somebody else. I'm interested in management. I want to run my own business, write my own rules, make a name for myself, and do it on my terms."

A year ago Diane was working as designer for a company that had to break into the big time, starting with the next season's line. If they could do it, they'd be on top; otherwise they'd go under. It was that tight a situation. Both partners in the company liked Diane's designs and saw her continuing to work for them as a backstage employee. But what she wanted was to emerge from backstage and start building her own design studio. She thought to herself, "The timing is great—right now. I hold all the cards. Without my designs they can't possibly produce the spring line in time, nor can they replace me in time to get that line done. This is a wonderful opportunity for me to come up with a plan that's to their advantage and mine."

Diane could have gone in and put a gun to her bosses' heads, threatening to pull out unless they set her up with a design studio she could manage. That would have created hostility and gotten her no further than springtime. Instead, she researched the firm's needs very carefully, to see how she could sweeten the pot for the partners while getting what she wanted. Diane came up with a meticulously itemized proposal. It encompassed a design fee for herself, and included the costs of leasing and setting up a separate studio, payroll, materials to produce samples and duplicates, the number of new designs she would produce per season, and the time periods required. She explained to the partners how their investment in setting up the studio would be to the company's advantage right now. She would take care of locating and leasing the space, get together a production staff, and work out all the administrative details. This would free the partners of the burdensome groundwork necessary to a new undertaking and let them use their energies instead to cash in quickly on the marketplace. She adds, "It also allowed us to work together in a new way. Before, when I was on their payroll, we were not dealing with each other as equals. I was just an employee. Now they began to take me seriously, to see me as much in a management capacity as in design."

Diane had her lawyer draw up a contract, with the payouts scheduled so that the company would not be placed in a bind and she would still realize a nourishing profit. That flexibility on her part also helped win her bosses' agreement to set her up in her own studio.

I should say, "her former bosses' agreement." Diane

and they are now peers professionally. She has her own separate design and production organization, which she manages, the company handles sales and distribution of the line, and it's a complete win/win situation.

The Big Hang-up: Asking for What You Want

Herein lies the rub in all our selling efforts, most especially when what we're selling is ourselves. Asking for a job, a raise, or anything else we want is painfully difficult. It's the one thing we don't know how to do, and resist doing by reflex. Asking is antithetical to everything we've learned as women, and the one area where we have no backlog of experience we can transfer to business skill. Everything else is there: giving people what they want, listening to what they say and don't say, reacting to situations, organizing projects, persuading. But when it comes to asking for something for ourselves, we have nothing we can convert into selling ability. All we know, from generations of conditioning, is that women are givers and that it's wicked to express our own needs. As a result, we retreat in panic from asking for anything for ourselves, quavering, "What if they say No? They'll hate me for asking. It's better never to have asked at all than to ask for something and not get it, or worse, to be despised."

The Myth of Asking by Magic

How often have you heard someone complain, "I am so angry with that man! I've worked for him night and day for three years and never once has he offered me a raise.

You'd think he could see for himself that I should be paid more for the hard work I do."

Sure he should. But how does he know? All he does is sign the paychecks on Fridays, he doesn't evaluate each one. And he's not your mommy, who was so sensitive to your wants she always gave whatever was in your mind before you had to ask for it. In other words, you have to let people know what you want, if you want to get it. Believing that you don't have to ask just because you hate asking is believing in magic, an illusion that won't pan out. The reality is, not asking means not getting. And not getting leads to brooding, and brooding leads to being angry because somebody didn't do what you secretly wanted them to do. Asking by magic—who needs it?

If you don't ask for what you want, unless you're working with a great mind reader you're never going to get it. Practice is needed.

The Biggest Hang-up: Asking for Money

"Lucre is filthy. The love of money is the root of all evil. Ladies never discuss money. Finances are a man's job. Cash is hard, women are soft." So goes the litany, and we are appalled when we have to ask for money for what we do. That's what prostitutes do. But money does count, and if you want it, it's a topic to tackle and become comfortable with once and for all. You have to change your thinking away from, "Clean money is the money I get from my father and my husband; dirty money is the money I have to ask for myself," so you can reach the stage Myra did when she finally got a solid career going. She says, "It is heaven to be getting all the money I want every week. For the first time I can do things for myself.

Take myself to dinner, furnish my apartment, buy clothes, have the things I need and the luxuries I don't need at all. And I don't have to depend on anyone else to do these things for me. It is heaven."

Reality: *Selling usually is about money.*

Money is business. It is the measure of the quality of wares and services. It is what changes hands in nearly all transactions, the end result of the selling process. Get used to the facts and make friends with them. Money *is* your friend, and it's what selling is usually all about. It signals the worth of your abilities, the extent you are in charge of yourself and situations. It bespeaks initiative and professionalism. Money is power and to be timid about asking for it is to automatically preclude advancement in your career. A job, a raise, a promotion, all the steps that mark you as a person of value carry with them the symbol of money. Unless you take money into account and become comfortable asking for what you are worth, that symbol and its ancillary benefits will not be conferred upon you.

Two points of view may help you become comfortable. One is that asking for money is nothing more than the barter system at work. It is what you receive in exchange for filling a need that somebody has. Barter is not aggressive or pushy or nasty. It is a kindly exchange, a safe and productive reality. And reality is the coin of every successful person.

The second way to make peace with asking for your money is to change the language in your head, translating *ask* to *offer*. When you ask for what you want, whether it's the signature on a sales contract or a raise, you are pointing out what you have and offering to provide it.

You are saying, in effect, "I can plan, organize, meet deadlines so expertly that your profits will increase if you accept my offer to put those abilities to work for you. In exchange, I expect you to reciprocate and compensate me for value received."

Reality: *If you don't ask for what you are worth, you probably won't get it.*

One of the problems I keep hearing voiced is the one Julie expresses as an anxiety. She says, "What I get anxious about is naming my price. I'm afraid to say to somebody, 'No, I want more.' What's worse for me is trying to come to terms in my mind with what my price is and what they will pay. I'm scared they'll say, 'No, we've decided we don't want you at all.' "

In general, women don't charge what they are worth. As you know, that is a major issue the women's movement has been addressing: equal pay for equal work. But the law won't cover everything for you. You have to have the courage to ask even if you're feeling scared and uncomfortable. You have to learn to acknowledge your worth despite your fear of asking for it.

Until you come to grips with the fact that you deserve to be compensated and that it's your right to ask for the money you earn, you'll keep giving out signals of unworthiness. Saying things like, "I think I deserve to be paid three hundred dollars," instantly betrays your uncertainty. Omit the "I think" and make your statement positive and sure. Drop the cutesy, little-girl approach. It's another clue that you're easy to get the better of, a signal people will take advantage of. Even a letter can tell tales on you. Here's a classic from the file marked, "Be Positive, for Lordsake."

> Virginia told me which apron you would like to have. I can put it straight "into production" and have it by the twenty-fourth for you. To make it easier for me, I ask people I deal with directly to please send a check before I send the apron so I don't have to hassle bills because I only deal with shops as a rule—and try to maintain a hard business attitude.
>
> The apron is $15 from me $25 plus tax at Saks, and *naturally* if you have a problem about it, it's all adjustable . . . good neighbor policy!

"To make it easier for me," "so I don't have to hassle bills"—cutsey-pooh. Talk straight! Look at that "*naturally*": Did you ever see such a giveaway? All those flowery little trills mean she just can't bear the idea of money. A real patsy.

Difficulty in acknowledging one's money's worth goes back to the social conditioning that tells us, falsely, that women are nice, money is dirty, and it's embarrassing to take money for what you do. Women have tended, therefore, to ask only for the bare necessities—enough to pay the grocery and transportation bills but not enough to cover their time and expertise. The plain business facts are these:

1. The economic system is structured so that time and talent have cash value. Rates and salaries depend on the value of your abilities and the time you devote to a job. As your proven track record for excellence becomes stronger, your value becomes greater and so do the sums you charge. Being timid about asking for what you are worth can only lead to dealing forever with the bargain hunters of the world, nickel-and-diming yourself to the poorhouse.

Selma learned that lesson fairly early in her career as

a marketing consultant. She'd established herself as a fund adviser whose recommendations made money for the six or eight companies that had engaged her. When a large corporation called on her to consult on a major new program, Selma knew her $150-a-day fee was no longer appropriate. "If I charge $200, will they pay it or hire somebody else? It seems so . . . bold to ask for so much money. I'll ask my accountant what he thinks I should do." The accountant thought she should be locked up. He pointed out, "You've proved that you're worth a lot of money to the companies that take your advice, and this one has already signaled that they believe in investing in your services. At this stage you ought to be setting your rates at $400 a day minimum, and escalate after that." He was right: Nobody questioned the $400 fee and Selma has since built a roster of high-paying clients who appreciate her worth and are willing to pay for what she does.

2. As you become stronger in your expertise and charge for it accordingly, you enhance your position because you are advertising that you are special and hard to get. In the same way that only a wealthy and discriminating few can pay for the superior Rolls Royce, there is cachet in your high-priced superiority. It's the same premise on which "the most expensive perfume in the world" is sold to a willing clientele over similarly excellent products.

When our company gives seminars for marketing people, I've found that offering the sessions as a free service results in a diffident audience. There's an attitude of "you get what you pay for." But when we charge for the seminars, the fee automatically signals that we are authorities and people pay attention to what we say.

You don't lose sales or jobs by charging what you are

worth. You build up a good reputation by dealing from your strength. All you have to lose are the jobs that cost you money.

3. Set your price realistically, and if it's higher than your prospect thinks he or she can afford, you have to be willing to hear No. With a No you can then either negotiate to a price you can live with or go on to sell your ability to another person. The point is not to fear asking what you're worth because you anticipate and dread losing the sale, and not to be stampeded into underselling yourself at bargain-basement rates. Either way makes you a loser.

You're apt to lose, too, if you're a high-priced achiever and settle into one of the traditional low-paying and crowded women's fields such as education, health care, merchandising, or publishing. From my own experience, I can tell you that there are profitable ways to transfer your skills into a higher-paying field. In the early 1960s my career was teaching improvisation to children at community centers and summer camps. The going rate was five dollars an hour, and that's what I got. Later in the sixties I brought the same skills to industry. I called what I did "market research," added a professional aspect by teaming up with a market researcher, and began earning the $125 hourly rate that industry paid. The skills I used were identical; it was simply a matter of transferring them to where the grass was greener. Anybody can do the same. If your ability is for sales and you have a real affinity for selling, you can sell pharmaceuticals as well as you can sell textbooks. I know a woman who started as a department store cosmetics salesperson and moved her skills and affinity into new product development for a cosmetics manufacturer. Another acquaintance who had been a low-salaried operating-room assistant has transferred her expertise and interest in health care to the high-paying area of consultancy in new hospital development. All you need is your ability, a lot of affinity, a bit of imagination, and the willingness to experiment.

How to Price Yourself Right

Establishing what you are worth can be done in a variety of ways. Ask around. Read books and trade journals. Research in every way possible to find out the going rates or salaries in the field you're interested in, at your level of accomplishment. There are lists, directories, articles, dozens of clues to current market value. If you're in a free-lance or service field where there is little or no industry documentation, ask both buyers and sellers what the going rate is in your part of the country. Keep in mind, though, that rates change from time to time and that some people you ask may have reason to shade their responses.

Be flexible, but within limits. And set those limits, mentally, before you go and ask for the job or the raise. Ask yourself, what do I think I should be paid for this, and what's the least I will accept? Then you will be prepared to negotiate from your initial offering, if need be, but will not find yourself discounting your price below realistic rock bottom.

If you do get into negotiation and your primary goal is the money, be prepared to lose or refuse a job if the price is too low for what your ability is worth. Just be sure, going in, that if you don't win the sale you have someplace else to go, or have enough money in the bank to tide you over. That's a wonderful position to be in because you come from the greatest possible strength when it's absolutely all right for you to lose.

How to Ask for What You Want: Clearly and with Confidence

To communicate what you want effectively, you must st on goal. You have to stay clear of hidden motivatio such as seeking approval, and abandon counterprodu tive behavior such as avoiding conflict or rejection.

The Dos of Asking

• Be direct. Ask for what you want without beatir around the bush or watering down your message with i relevant issues.

• Be clear. Ask for what you want specifically: so mar dollars or such and such a position, and back yo request with clearly perceivable reasons why granting would be mutually favorable.

• Be calm. Apologetic nervous giggles, distractin jerky gestures, a tense voice and tentative inflectio negate what you want to communicate.

• Rehearse before you ask. Role-play and role-pla with a partner, so that you are comfortable in the scen you're about to enter and have command of the scenari Think of yourself as an actress about to appear before first-night audience and prepare by practicing all th lines and gestures. Let your partner play the devil's a vocate, so you'll be prepared for the objections that ma arise. Good preparation makes it easier to make th good first impression, and this is the *you* your prospe will either applaud or walk out on. You *can* go back agai if you blow the first meeting, but it's the hard way.

The Don'ts of Asking

• Don't apologize or downplay yourself. ("I'm sorry t take up your time with something unimportant . . .")

- Don't obfuscate your goal. ("I came to ask for a promotion to head buyer but maybe you think I should be at branch store.")
- Don't stray from your agenda. ("I want to take three weeks instead of two for my vacation. By the way, did I show you the snapshots I took two years ago when I was in Capri?")
- Don't clown or neutralize what you say out of nervousness. ("Uh, I want to talk with you about my salary ha-ha-ha.")
- Don't be flirtatious. ("I want to discuss my fee for this assignment. A girl has to be paid for putting out, if you know what I mean.")

The Selling Game Do and Don't Playhouse

Here are two scenes from a play called *Yours for the Asking*. The show will never hit Broadway—in fact, it'll never get out of this book. The dialogues exist only to illustrate some of the dos and don'ts of asking.

Scene I. A new division is being formed by your company. You want to be the director, so you will rehearse one of these three scripts.

Dialogue A: Umm, I wouldn't turn down the opportunity of being director. I'd be willing to work in the new division if you can find somebody to cover what I do now.

Dialogue B: I guess I'd be interested in heading the division. If I could make the time. It's sort of related to what I do now, isn't it? I suppose it would be a good challenge for me.

Dialogue C: I am extremely enthusiastic about what this division will be doing. I've had a lot of experience in work of this sort, and know a lot of people in the field who can assist us in performing the work. In fact, one of the ke men at our major financial resource is friend of mine and he has already told m that he will cooperate with me on seeing th the division is successful. Also, I know that work well with the staff here; you've com mented yourself how productivity an morale have gone up since I've been i charge of the department where I am now At this point, I could readily train somebod to take over my responsibilities at the sam time I'm helping to start up the new divisior I know I could help you do this thing righ and I'd really like to take on the directorship

Scene II. You are applying for a job you want bu you're not sure if the salary being offered is reasonabl for your worth and your needs. You want to ear $25,000.

Dialogue A: Well, to take the job I'd have to get mor than the $18,000 I'm earning now.

Dialogue B: I hate to sound pushy, but I have to know about the salary before I can decide if could work to fill your needs. I couldn't tak a job for less than . . . how does $20,000 o $25,000 sound to you?

Dialogue C: To assume the responsibilities you've out lined, I'd have to be paid enough to make i worthwhile for me to leave my present job. have built up a lot of credentials there and in prior positions, and have shown that I can d the kind of work we're talking about, ex pertly and profitably. I know the value of my ability and the extent of your needs. They match beautifully. At $25,000 we could work together very well.

Curtain

Director, enters stage left. Holds large placard to audience]

Always speak clearly, calmly, and confidently
Always get your act together before you go onstage
And always use Script C.

Ask Right, and Ask the Right Person

You can do all the right things and still not get what you're asking for if you're not asking the right person. You have to know where the power is, who really has the decision-making ability, or your efforts will be in vain. Prior research will usually clue you to who the right person is, though there'll be times when only trial and error will lead you to the decision-maker. Don't be irritated or complain when that happens. A lot of people have turf to protect or ego to inflate. Your job is to keep everybody on your side and let them help you find the person who can say, "I need you and I can buy."

Kay found this out when she was hunting for her very first job. A half-dozen times she went into offices and spoke with the receptionist or secretary. A half-dozen times she heard, "There aren't any jobs open in our sales department." When she began to hear about friends who were getting sales jobs at the same companies she'd called on, it dawned on her that the people she'd spoken to were either uninformed or didn't want another attractive female on the premises. Kay learned fast that to get action, she had to go where the action is—to the sales director or president of the company and not a person in lower management position who couldn't say Yes or No i he/she wanted to.

Nancy's had many similar experiences and perhap always will, though the longer she's a free-lance magazin journalist the more she knows about who's really who. I often happens that she has no choice but to take her ar ticle ideas to an assistant editor, a novice who's all enthu siasm and praise, but never assigns an article becaus he/she really doesn't have the power. Or the experienc to know when it's all right to admit it. Protocol require that Nancy go through the motions; what she's learned t do is remain cheerful and cooperative, and find ways t reach the editor with the ability to buy so she can sell, no just have good ideas that go nowhere.

Now for the Finale . . .

Now you know what you're after: which job, how mucl raise, what promotion. You've pinpointed the prospec you'll talk to. You've researched and have a bank of in formation. You've built a chain of contacts. So far, you'v made all the right moves. You're almost ready for action Read on.

10

Sex and Selling

If you're good-looking, men deal with you one way. They smile and work at being attractive themselves. If you're not good-looking, they come on another way. It's a tricky thing if you come on strong sexually. Men get very wary because they can see that you're using your sexual skills instead of your professional skills.

Women have a big advantage in selling to men: We have the choice of being women or being just people. Men who sell to men don't have that option; their sexual roles don't matter. As a woman coming in with every disadvantage, with no history in business, I'm willing to use any edge I've got.

How you handle sex in selling is a matter of personal style: whether you rely on the curves and angles of your femininity or decide never to mix business and sex.

You may or may not be offended at the thought of

using sex to sell. The fact is that your sexual persona is part of you, and even if you decide to ignore it, it still exists. Furthermore, others may decide not to ignore it, in which case sex can work against you unless you understand what is happening. Most of the successful women in business have decided that as long as their sexuality will be taken into account anyway, they would rather be the ones in control of how and to what extent it is used. No judgments need be made about sex in selling, because there is no right or wrong. It's simply a matter of individual business philosophy, methods, and strategy.

The Roles Women Play

How you handle sex in business is a reflection of how you lead your life, because how you live is how you sell. It's a transfer of facets of your personality from private to business life.

There are four traditional roles women play—in life and in business. Whichever is your essential type, you'll find there are times you will switch roles to accommodate a situation.

The Mother is supportive, encouraging, likes to reassure others. She is a problem-solver who likes to take charge and organize things.

The Child goes through life looking for someone to take care of her. In business, she can be sweet and seemingly pliant, giggly and girlish, or so insistent in asking for what she wants that people find it easier to give in to her than to resist.

The Sex Object relies heavily on her wiles and physical attractiveness to get what she wants. She tends to be manipulative, overtly or indirectly.

The Person is a relatively new figure on the business scene. She is straightforward, direct, and genderless in that sex is not part of her selling technique.

None of us is totally one type or another; we all switch and combine roles, consciously or unconsciously, to meet our own and others' needs. For example, you may be dealing with an Old School gentleman who is unaccustomed to working with women and is uncomfortable. It would be better to adapt your style to accommodate his and swim with the tide than to fight his image of you as a belle. One way to meet the situation would be to assume the conventional trappings. If yours is a dinner meeting, bringing along an escort would symbolize that you're a sweet and womanly type, not the high-powered independent he fears. With this kind of client or customer, you can build his confidence in you over the years, educating him gradually until he accepts you on your own terms.

Obviously, you'd adapt other roles or combinations of roles to the needs of other kinds of clients.

Handling the Almost-a-Mother Role

If there's one thing the Old School type of man can't handle, it's the sight of a pregnant woman working. He thinks you should be home taking care of yourself for the sake of the child. You shock him, but you can handle his discomfort by quiet reason. Talk about your pregnancy if the subject comes up. Ask about his experiences with children. Don't be defensive. I'll tell you what I said when it came up with me. I was six months pregnant and calling on an ultraconservative gentleman in Texas. He didn't want to buy what I was selling because he was afraid that I wouldn't be able to follow up with service. He expected that I'd stay at home with the baby after it was born, and he said he was sure that's what my husband expected, too. I explained that undoubtedly that was what he would like to see for his wife, but that my husband felt differently: He wanted me to go on with my career and, since we both felt that way, I would most assuredly be on hand to service his account.

Sexism in Business

There is sex in business, and there is sexism. It is unrealistic to assume that all resistance to working women has magically melted away. Some men deeply resent working with women, and others are threatened by it. Some men don't resent women at all, but see them as sexual objects or fragile commodities, to be treated gallantly and not taken seriously.

How do you handle these situations? Do you barge ahead, trying to convert these men to your political views about working women? Not if you want to win the sale and keep a friendship. When you're selling, you're working to get agreement and the last thing you want to do is get into an argument or reinforce the image of feminists as militant. Unless you are truly being harrassed and must therefore let it be known that there is legal recourse you may seek, a far better solution is to answer sexist remarks with calm and confidence. "My husband approves of my working and my child is well cared for," will satisfy the man who tells you you ought to be home nurturing your husband and Junior. Or when the M.B.A. after your name is ignored and your typing speed is questioned instead, you can make your point quietly with a response like, "My training as an administrator will be of enormous benefit to your company; my typing is for personal use only." And the type who calls you "Honey" can be taken care of with an unemotional, "Perhaps you didn't catch my name. It's Mary Smith."

Often just working with a woman is enough to convince a man that she is a person of value, when no amount of talk could change his mind. Through professionalism, you can take the sting out of working with a diehard misogynist by defeating his expectations of what working women are like. You might say that this is using sex to overcome sexism.

Sexual Encounters of the Selling Kind

Even if you have chosen not to use your sexuality in business, sexual encounters are going to arise. They may be unexpected, unusual, or just awkward. Especially if you are a beginner in business, it helps to know how other women have dealt with their experiences. Nicole, a chic, vivacious account executive, tells how one loaded situation was defused:

> I was out of town, in Pittsburgh, giving a presentation together with a colleague from another company—a man with whom I'd done this sort of thing for years. Our relationship was strictly on the good-friend level, easy and comfortable. When we left the presentation we found there was a blizzard in progress and all the planes were

grounded. It was urgent for each of us to get back to New York for appointments in the morning, so we dashed for the railroad station. As it turned out, the only train available was a sleeper, and there was only one compartment to be had. We both stood there thinking, "What should I do?" We turned to each other, and he said, "It's your choice." As far as I was concerned, there was only one choice: "Who's going to take the lower berth?" My big need was to get back to New York; the sexual implications of the situation had nothing to do with reaching that goal.

Beth, a good-looking blonde in her middle thirties, encountered a far more awkward situation and managed to handle it with grace:

> Another woman and I were hostessing the entertainment suite our company had set up for an industry convention. The party we had put on was very successful, and we were sitting around afterward discussing it with our employer, the president of the company. As she and I were leaving, the president called to me and said, "Beth, wait a minute, will you? I'd like to see you about something." He was rather drunk, but I thought harmless. And he was the boss. So I returned. He said, "Wait here, please. I'll be right with you."
>
> He went into one of the bedrooms and closed the door. Two minutes later, he emerged—stark naked! I was absolutely aghast. All I knew was I wanted to get out of there instantly. I bolted from the suite and raced down the hotel corridor to the elevator. He raced after me—still naked. I was wild with panic. Then, just as the elevator door opened so I could escape, I heard the door to the suite slam shut. There was poor Arthur, trapped in public in the absolute buff. I had to think fast. There were three choices. I could get into the elevator and just disappear. I could take the elevator to the lobby and send a bellboy up with a key. Or I could fling Arthur my wrap so he could

cover himself, and then flee. Out of charity, I settled on the third option, which covered his ass, so to speak, at the same time it got me off the scene.

For three months afterward, Arthur barely spoke to me. His embarrassment was not surprising, and I let the matter ride until I found a way to bring up the episode casually. By then I thought what had happened was hilarious, and my laughter relieved Arthur of his guilt. We have long since returned to our former business relationship, in spite of what could have been an untidy sexual escapade.

When Sex Is Part of Selling

Sure, I use sex to sell, the social sexual approach of female wiles. It disturbs me to resort to it, but it's worked my whole life. I've had men approach me sexually and I just keep up the tease act. I've made innumerable sales because the guy didn't want to disappoint poor little me. Sometimes I say to myself, "You really are a no-good prostitute, Janet." I don't know what the answer is, but I'll take advantage of anything I can get. Probably if I had to support my children and myself totally, I wouldn't play around and tease because it would be too risky.

There are an infinite number of ways sex is used or accommodated in business, as these examples show. Some women are obvious, and even determined. Others don't use sex to get ahead but are willing that it be part of a business relationship.

There's an editor who calls me three or four times a year, when he gets in a jam and needs an article researched and written quickly. He's done this for several years, and those were the only times we ever saw each other—until one day about a year and a half ago. We

> were having one of our infrequent editorial conferences over lunch, we both had a few drinks, one thing led to another and next thing I knew we were at my place having fantastic sex. He left, and I didn't hear from him again. A couple of months later, I had a terrific yen to get into bed with him again. So I called and asked if he could come over that night. He knew exactly what was on my mind, and again the sex was fantastic.
>
> Since then, I've called him whenever I feel like having sex. He comes over, we go to bed, and that's all there is to it. He never calls me, it's not really an affair. I guess you'd say he's my stud. I take it back about his never calling me. He does, when he needs a rush article. And on those conferences we're still strictly business, each of us intent only on the job that's to be done. The sex never interferes.

There is a danger, though, of getting involved with the people you work with, and the danger is not necessarily that you will get hurt, as Leslie, a business consultant, points out:

> I've been attracted to people I've worked on projects with, and I've found that having sex with them just complicates things. A lot of times the magnetism has to do with the excitement of the project itself. When the project's over there's nothing there. One time I was on a six-month project, and I was having an affair with my co-worker, Tom. I was having a less pleasant affair with our client; we had a personality conflict. The only way to bail out the project successfully was to have Tom take over as the client contact, which he did. But he lost respect for my professionalism because we were too intimate at the personal level. The project never went well after that.

Probably the most important factor in combining sex and business is to be very clear in your head about what you are doing. Mixing sex and business won't work in the long run if you feel guilty or abused by your actions, or if you aren't willing to cope with the situation that gets out of hand, as happened to Irma:

> As a manufacturer's showroom manager, I get to meet and sell to a great many men from out of town. One, whom I'll call Steve, is from St. Louis. We met when he came into town on a buying trip. He was a new account for us, and when he saw the quality and scope of our line of machine tool equipment, he purchased carloads. The commissions to me were fantastic. I'd never seen that much money all at once in my life. Not only that, I could see that his potential as a big buyer could mean that as long as he was my customer, I wouldn't have to worry about money. I mean it: His first order put me into a whole other tax bracket.
>
> In addition to being my ticket to financial freedom, Steve was extremely attractive. He was good-looking, a gentleman, meticulously groomed, well-mannered, and articulate. So when he asked me if I would dine with him that evening, I accepted. We went to a fine restaurant, and during dinner he told me a little about himself. I'm a very sympathetic person and a lot of people tell me their personal problems, so I wasn't surprised when he began talking about his mentally ill wife and the troubles he was having with his teen-age son. We were enjoying each other's company, and after dinner we went back to my apartment so we could continue to talk. That's *all* we did. We talked until two in the morning and when he left, I felt that I'd established a good relationship with a valuable customer with whom I'd be doing business for a long time. I liked him. And I *loved* the big commissions I could see in my future.
>
> About a week later, I got a phone call at ten at night. It was Steve, calling to say hello. By the time I got off the phone it was eleven-thirty and I had listened to a lot more

of what was going on in his personal life. I didn't mind; I enjoy helping people by listening.

The next week he called again and told me he was sending me another substantial order for our machine tool products. Then he talked for another hour and a half about his wife, his son, his enormous home, his private plane, and his plans for a trip to Europe. I was beginning to know him quite well.

By the following month, he was calling me every night, and now the conversations began to include me. He said he found me very attractive. and he enjoyed being able to throw so much business my way. Mind you, he hadn't even made a pass that one time we were together. I was beginning to realize something weird was going on. It didn't take much longer to find out what it was. The phone calls got more and more personal, until he finally eased into what he'd been after all along: sex by phone. That's what turned him on. I'd heard of that kind of thing before, but never experienced it firsthand. I didn't like it; it made me uncomfortable and it didn't do a thing for my libido. But he was insistent, and by now he was in the driver's seat and I had a dilemma. If I cut off the telephone sex, I'd cut off all those glorious commissions because he wouldn't need me for what he really wanted. If I continued to be his sex partner via long distance, I'd have to keep putting up with his interminable and by now irritating late-night calls. Which did I want to live with? I decided the money was the most important thing to me, and if I had to get it by using sex, that's what I'd do.

You are less likely to get into trouble if you know exactly how you stand on the subject of mixing sex and business. Some women need to work things out on a situation-by-situation basis; others are startled into an evaluation of their feelings by a random incident. Sometimes women are not even aware of using sexuality until someone points out the role it plays for them, as in Thelma's case:

> I am attracted to other women, and ever since a rather humiliating incident, I've made it a rule to keep my personal life separate from business. It changed my dress style, too. Until this incident occurred, I wore my blouses open to the point where you could see everything down to the rib cage. I was dressed this way at a meeting with a woman client I was sexually attracted to, and she was giving me a hard time over paying for a job I'd done for her. I was trying with all the guile I have to coax her into paying, and at the same time I must have been using some inter-body language she picked up. All of a sudden she interrupted what I was saying and snapped, "What are you trying to sell me—your drawings or your breasts?" It came out of the blue, and I was embarrassed that I'd been so blatant. I backed off immediately and learned a good lesson about keeping sex in its place.

There is always room to reevaluate your attitude about using sexuality in business. For a long time Phyllis thought she was comfortable with her sexual role, but she is beginning to reconsider her style:

> At my office they treat me like a female and I respond the way they want me to. They're manipulating me and I know it, but I act out the stereotype the way they want to see me. It's a lot easier for me than taking on the whole system and it wins points, even though it's not my disposition to cross my legs at the ankles and be demure and sweet. What troubles me is I haven't changed things for my sixteen-year-old daughter. She copies me, doing all the "aren't you big, strong, and clever" tricks. I hate to watch her.

Rejecting Sexual Overtures

If you have decided to rule out using sex, you still have to be prepared for sexual approaches from men. Acting the role of a Person helps, but is very subtle and can sometimes be seen as a challenge. Most women use one of two styles to handle unwelcome approaches: the direct and the indirect parry. Here is how Naomi handled a sexual overture directly:

> The vice-president of a hotel chain was interviewing me for the project of redesigning their function rooms. One of the assignments was to name each room after a famous woman. He said, "You'll have the job if . . ." And then he leered suggestively. I'm through being upset; I just called him on it. I said, "I'm not sure of your meaning. I'd get the job if what? If I come up with good names? Or do you have something else in mind?" I've found that if I'm very direct and call men on this issue, they get embarrassed, or they get the message and lay off.

Handling these situations indirectly works well, too, especially if you can keep repeating your message without losing your temper. Roberta, who is both spectacularly attractive and thoroughly professional, tells how she has managed:

> This happens to me time and time again. A manager or vice-president will meet me on a sales call I'm making and come out with some innuendo like, "Aren't you too pretty to be so high-powered?" Then he'll go on to say, "What do you do to relax?" I'll describe some of my hobbies and he'll keep pushing: "What do you say we get together a little later? Being in business for yourself, you must have a lot of free time. Maybe we could get something together at three or four o'clock." I always smile and make believe it was a very funny joke on his part. I'll say,

"Thanks very much, but I never do that sort of thing without a contract in my hand." Or sometimes I won't comment at all. I'll just laugh and go on to what I was going to say next, which usually brings it right back to business.

Doing Business with Men Outside the Office

Another time when sex can become a factor in business relationships is when you transact business outside the office, something all successful women must learn to do. Men have always appreciated the value of business conducted in a social setting and since time began have been solidifying business ties if not actually signing contracts on golf courses and tennis courts, in private clubs and over meals. Now it is our turn to master the techniques.

At the same time we learn that it is useful to conduct business outside the office, we must also learn the how-to's. Done right, these situations can be highly effective. Mishandled, they can make a male client feel ill at ease.

Taking a man out of his office works especially well because it takes him away from his command post. It puts him on neutral ground, where you can take charge. Further, it eliminates interruptions of your agenda by the telephone and staff.

It is important in these encounters that you be in control, that you stay on goal and accomplish the business you have set out to accomplish. There are a number of power things you can do to keep the reins in your hands. For instance, you're the one who should bring up business, usually over dessert or toward the end of the meal. You can also suggest what items on the menu are particularly good, and let your guest do his own ordering if he is more comfortable that way. You should definitely be the one to pick up the tab. After all, you are the person who is doing the selling and making a profit, so you should be paying. Here are three of the ways to arrange for paying the bill so that money never crosses the table and your male guest is not made uneasy:

- Call ahead and instruct the maître d'hôtel to hold the bill so you can take care of it privately. At the right time, you can excuse yourself from the table, as if you were going to the ladies' room, and take care of the check out of sight of your guest.
- Join a private club where money never changes hands and only members' signatures are accepted, so there's no way a man can pick up the check.
- Use a credit card so that cash or dollar amounts are never embarrassingly visible. If the subject of paying comes up, you can say that you are working on an expense account. It will be true even if the bill comes to you personally, because the expense will be your investment in winning a sale.

What to Do When Drink Time Arrives

This is a concern for a great many women. They're afraid to look like a poor sport or prissy, but they know mixing business and alcohol can lead to trouble. Most of the successful women we spoke with handle it very simply: They don't drink on the job because they want to be sure they stay in command. What they do instead, so as to be graceful and not leave the man in the awkward spot of having to drink alone, is to order a Virgin Mary, a Perrier and lime or, at most, a white wine spritzer. Just be sure you can handle what you take on and you'll be all right.

Sex and Money—Paying for What You Get

Nothing comes without a price. If you decide to mix business and sex, then you should be aware that some men may expect the price to be sex. And while it is one thing to use the sexual aspect of your personality in selling, you most surely are not obligated to repay business favors with a romp in the hay.

However, when somebody does something for you, you are obligated to pay for it. That's a simple business fact. When a friend, male or female, gives you a business lead or offers to sell your service or product for you, you are expected to repay that person with thanks, a favor, referrals, or hard cash in the form of a commission, a finder's fee, or whatever the two of you decide on.

The best way to avoid any misunderstanding about what the payment for a favor will be is to discuss it directly. In my industry as in many others, new-business leads are a way of life. What I like to do when somebody gets me a new client is draw up a written contract confirming the 10 percent or other commission we've decided on as fair payment. And then I keep the other person informed as to what's happening with the new client, so as not to leave him in limbo about his commission; it could be ninety days before I get paid and can send along 10 percent of the check. Keeping the person informed keeps him happy. It also keeps him hustling for me because he knows that it pays. And it gets me off the hook of being beholden in any way, including the idea of sexual favors.

Reality: Sell *is the four-letter act you perform every day—despite or because of your sex.*

11

The Importance of Dress Rehearsals

My partners and I have formed the habit of always thinking, ahead of every meeting, "If we could write the script of what's going to happen—of what we *want* to happen and of what *can* happen—how would the script go?" Then we sit down and write it six ways to Sunday. We decide what the goal of the meeting is to be: to get a definite Yes or No decision, or to get an appointment for another meeting. We work out in advance all the possible variations and nuances that can make or break it for us. We try to think of every detail, so we won't find ourselves grappling with unpleasant surprises. This kind of preparation has become automatic with us. It's amazing how it's increased our effectiveness.

Successful people know exactly what they're going to do before they do it. Orchestra leaders follow scores, architects build according to blueprint, ballplayers have practice sessions—and people who sell well, sell according to well-rehearsed plan. If you think rehearsing is a difficult and time-consuming exercise, think of it this way: In the same time and energy you'd spend complaining and worrying about the presentation you're going to make, you could educate yourself instead, and help guarantee profit and productivity.

Being prepared for what you want to make happen at a sales presentation is winning a major portion of the game before it begins. It arms you with confidence; lets you present yourself, or your product or service, in the best possible light. It puts you in command—of yourself, your fear, and the selling situation itself. Rehearsal is a power factor, one of the most effective tools you can use for success.

Setting the Scene for Rehearsal

An obvious simile to rehearsing a sales presentation is rehearsing a play. The compositions are the same: Each has a cast of characters, costumes, setting, props, theme, acting style, dialogue, timing, and an audience. Thinking in terms of theatrical production, then, let's run through the elements of rehearsal for success.

The details of your production are important: how you look, where you are, what you say. But it's the sum of these parts that has impact—the effect of the production, not the pieces that go into it. What follows are guidelines, because there is no single correct way of presenting yourself. You just have to be aware of what *your* details add up to. If you're a person whose signature is wearing blue jeans and sandals, and it's important to you personally to wear them even at a presentation to an ultraconservative prospect, you're entitled. That's you. Your costume isn't going to make or break the sale, but you are going to have to work harder to convince your prospect of your credibility, having foregone that particular item of support for your professionalism. If you're a helter-skelter type and it seems false to you to suddenly put your office in clinical order for the benefit of a certain prospect, so be it. You'll have to make up the lost points created by an untidy setting by being strong in other aspects of your presentation.

The Casting Session

The star is you. Or you and your team, if you work together with associates. The audience, your client or customer, is the partner you work with regularly, or a friend you can call on to help. It's very important to have someone else play opposite you, rather than trying to imagine the audience's reaction in your head. You need another person's mind and voice to respond to you, negatively and positively, to come up with arguments you might not think of yourself, and to provide analysis and suggestions.

Establish who each character is. The client or customer you'll be playing to may be conservative, hard-nosed, easygoing, flip, mature, insecure, or any of the human varieties that abound. You're one up if you are already familiar with your prospect's personality or can find it out by asking people who've dealt with him or her. If you're going to be facing an unknown quantity, do some digging in advance, so you will at least be informed about the self-image of the company he or she represents. You can study the firm's annual reports, read news articles at the public library, ask the company's public relations department for copies of the principals' speeches and public statements, or even buy a share of stock so you'll have personal access to inside information.

By all means, use a credit rating organization and ask other suppliers, if possible, to find out if you're going to be romancing a person or firm that pays its bills, before you waste your time and energy making a pitch.

Whatever your prospect's type, you need to know how to deal with him or her. With your buddy enacting the role, you'll discover how to use your own style to advantage. You'll also become aware of how you appear to your prospect. Frances, a boutique owner, says that the process of stepping back and seeing herself as if she were on stage has helped her identify and then strengthen what it is about herself that customers respond to best. "I think people pick up clues when you're not being direct with them or are devious in any way. I'm naturally a straightforward person and I try to project that directness in a casual way. I find that my style lets me establish rapport with customers without putting them off."

Chris is a state representative who's been elected to office three times. She says every election year is another sales campaign, and every address is a pitch. "My presentation style is to play the teacher. I think of myself as an expert in government administration, and I'm able to project that expertise so that people trust and believe in my authority."

Ellen had to learn to temper her naturally easygoing style. She felt it inappropriate to her functions as director of a national fund-raising organization. "In fact," she adds, "the way I come on when I'm not thinking about it would be out of place in many kinds of business situations. It implies a certain familiarity that should not be there. Especially if it's a first interview with somebody, I tone down my style at least until my professional credentials are well established. The rule of thumb I've developed is that assuming familiarity is never appropriate."

The creative director of a small advertising agency explains the effectiveness of team style, where one member's personality balances and augments the others'. She says, "There are three of us who own our agency. Jackie's the president, Sue is the account manager, and I'm the creative director. When we're pitching a new client, Jackie will be the peacemaker—the arbitrator who jumps in with compromise solutions when Sue and I seem to disagree, and who makes the concessions that move stalled negotiations along. She comes off as the reliable party who'll supervise every nickel and dime of the client's budget to make sure it's sensibly spent. Sue, the one who'll be working directly with the client, combines her professional comprehension of advertising with a naturally amiable personality. What clients get from her is a feeling of trust and friendship. They trust her business acumen and feel at ease with the nonintimidating way she gets them to do what's good for them. Me, I get away with being a little dotty, a little wild—the 'typical creative loon' who's fun to be with because I'm different from the business people they see every day. I'm the audacious creature they can count on to somehow produce the offbeat and consistently effective advertising that is our agency's hallmark. With the three of us presenting ourselves as a unit, what the clients see is an agency they can profit from; a team that will give them the common sense, dependability, financial responsibility, camaraderie, hand-holding, and terrific creative juice they need. I'm not at all sure any of us could carry off a client pitch as well individually as we do when we act as a team."

Presentation Style from a Prospect's Point of View

A corporate president told me of an experience he had not long ago, when he was interviewing a number of women for the position of executive assistant. He says, "It was a parade of characters. First, I got gabby Gladys. I'd known Gladys years ago when she'd been a secretary in another department. This trip, she presumed upon that acquaintance. Sailed into my office all hail-fellow-howzit-going. Opened up the meeting with reminiscences about the good old days. 'Boy, I was born to be your assistant,' she informed me, without even asking what the job was all about. She was busy wisecracking, even told a dirty joke, didn't bother to recognize my status or my needs; just whooped it up, as it were. It was overkill and needless to say, she killed her own chances.

"The next one said to me, after I'd laid out what the responsibilities would be, 'Why should I take this job?' I answered, 'I'm not going to tell you why you should take this job,' and as far as I was concerned, the interview was over.

"Character number three was terribly glib. One of the types I never hire. They anticipate what they think you want to hear and nozzle it at you. 'I'm just fascinated by your industry.' I'll ask them, 'What about hours?' 'Oh, hours never bother me at all. It doesn't bother me if I work holidays. I'll be here as long as it takes me to do the job.' Nonsense. It bothers everybody if they have to work on Christmas. These glib types oversell themselves in every way: references on a résumé that don't check out, exaggerations to the point of untruth about what they've actually done. And usually they babble so much I'm afraid that babble will turn into gossip if I hire them.

"The winning interview was with a young lady I'd also known previously. That almost worked against her because I'd known Peggy as a finger-popping, jazzy girl who's always a little too flip. That's OK when you're having a drink after work, but I had my doubts about how she'd work out in an office situation with serious responsibilities. Surprise. She came to the interview in a dress, not her standard blue jeans. Her demeanor was very serious. She handed me her résumé, saying, 'Maybe you don't know all the things I've done.' Then she addressed what she knew was the problem: 'I know you think I'm a person who'd be playing *Laugh-In* all the time. I want to tell you that when the chips are down and I have a job to do, I do that job and never mind anything else.' That earnestness plus the good checkouts on her résumé convinced me she was the person to hire."

Wardrobing the Star

> I used to dress poorly, come in late, not express clearly what I could do but expect people to figure it out as I bumbled along. I thought it was their problem. It wasn't. It was mine. What I had to learn was to practice and rehearse everything beforehand. To present myself so my appearance wouldn't get in the way. To be very clear what it is I'm selling to people, so they don't have to work hard to find out. To prethink everything so that I'm always ahead of the client and can steer the discussion toward my own ends.

The first impression you make on a person is one that will persist in his or her image of you, so it certainly pays to rehearse your presentation costume right down to the briefcase or portfolio you'll carry. Packaging yourself ight is as important in selling as packaging a cereal box r a lipstick: When people see something that appeals to hem, they want to buy. Therefore, the way you dress hould not only be in keeping with your own style—whether it's conservative, arty, chic, or elegant—it should e in keeping with your prospect's style of business and ersonal point of view. The clue to how to dress for a neeting is the same as for what you wear at a party or ootball game: Be appropriate.

Bobbie, a stockbroker who deals in corporate portfo-os, says what she wears depends on the level of the per-on she's seeing. "If it's not a high-up person, I don't verdo my look because it would threaten them. After all, elling is relating to people. For high-level executive neetings I pull out all the good jewelry, the designer suit nd shoes, the very expensive silk blouse. If I'm going to conservative firm or to see somebody in a small town where conspicuous consumption is frowned upon, I'll eave off the jewelry and pare down to simplicity. The ook is always elegant, nonetheless; it shows that I'm a erson who's arrived. Sometimes I'll choose a tailored suit n a subdued color and sometimes I'll wear fabrics and hades that are soft and feminine. It depends on who I'm eeing and how I want him or her to see me. I always arry a good leather briefcase and purse, and keep every-hing in them well organized so I won't be caught fum-bling among lipsticks and spare pantyhose in search of business cards or brochures. I even write down, in ad-vance, what I'm going to wear and what things I'll take with me on an appointment, so I'll be sure that what I want is in the closet and not at the cleaner's or cobbler's."

Janice puts it another way. She says, "Selling is always being what it is I represent, and always represent-ing what it is I do and am. If I'm selling professionalism and quality, I always have to be those things. I have to be a class act. I have to be organized and have quality material in my presentation. I can't afford anything slipshod in my appearance. I am very careful that my grooming is impeccable, and that my material is as perfectly organized as it is perfect in content. I pay as much attention to not having runs in my hose or spots on my dress as I do to showing work that is excellent, right down to the spelling and punctuation. I feel strongly that I have to be on every minute, because people buy an image as much as they buy a service or product.

"It happens that most of my clients are very conservative. They're in the financial community, so I always wear a skirt or a dress. If I'm wearing a skirt, I try to wear a jacket or vest, something to tie it together, instead of just a skirt and blouse. I try not to look like a little girl. For one thing, I'm young and *looking* young takes away from my authoritativeness. For another, I'm big, so I can't carry off cutesy stuff anyway. I'm careful about colors: I choose the ones that are tasteful and dignified, like burgundies and rust, even though I personally prefer bright reds, yellows, and blues. And if there's a choice between something that's fashionable and something that's serviceable, I'll choose the fashionable thing to wear. I sell in a tailored suit, even though I might really feel like wearing pants and an overblouse that day. I'll wear a dress in the new billowy style, rather than a dress I have from two years ago that might be more comfortable, because I know people will buy an image even when they don't know a thing about fashion. They pick up the sense that this person is sharp and with-it. I don't spend a lot of money on clothes or pay attention to labels, but I'm conscious that the impression I make is very important."

Nearly all of the successful women you'll see carry a

urse for their personal things and an attaché case, briefase, or portfolio for their business papers and products. t's wise to invest in expensive, well-made bags and cases; n addition to representing you as a person of quality and liscernment, they will last and look well for years. Keep hem polished and cared for at all times—ready to appear nstage in gleaming condition.

The Props

Your props are the selling tools of your trade. Your busiiess card, résumé, portfolio, and other material reflect vhat it is you do and your style of doing it. Rehearsing vhich props belong in a specific presentation gives you he advantage of having time to select or create the exact ools that will sell for you in that situation.

Here is a checklist that will help you review your rops inventory:

Business cards. Your card, like your letterheads, is *you* vhen you're not around, and you should invest in profesional and tasteful layout, typeface, and stock. Include our name, company and title if you have one, address nd telephone where you can be reached or where a mesage can be received. Keep a supply of business cards in our purse and briefcase at all times; you never know vho you're going to meet, or when.

Résumé. Always carry at least three résumés, in case our prospect has a colleague who can use you or wants n extra copy for the files. Tailor your résumé according o the situation. Several women I've worked with have as nany as five standing versions of their résumé, each eared to aspects of the fields they're interested in. And if their standing résumé doesn't fit a new situation, they'r ready to whip up additional versions that accent activitie and accomplishments in that particular field, and th eliminate or abbreviate irrelevancies. Tailor your résum but keep it honest. People really do check them out.

Credentials. A variety of materials falls under th heading of credentials. Select those that apply to you a this point, and add others if and when they become perti nent.

PORTFOLIO: Especially if you are in a creative fiel the only way a prospect knows what you can do is to sho him or her what you have done. Collect tear sheets, re prints, samples of everything you are proud of. Assembl them in an organized manner and showcase them in nea manageable form. Rehearse what you will bring to eac specific meeting, selecting what is relevant to your pros pect's needs to prevent having to wade through reams c papers during the interview in an attempt to find th samples that will sell.

PUBLICITY AND LETTERS OF PRAISE: Be prepared t present evidence of the positive things other people hav said of you, your product, your work. As with a portfoli of samples, assemble your publicity credentials in an or derly, easy-to-view collection.

PROMOTIONAL BROCHURES AND STATISTICAL IN FORMATION: In most cases these will be pieces you wi leave behind, for review by your prospect after you hav made your presentation. Know in advance what it is you' want him or her to have in his/her keeping. In addition t well-written, well-designed brochures and statistical fac ıd figures, you may want to leave publicity reprints, let-·rs of recommendation, samples of your product and, :rtainly, your business card.

VISUAL AIDS: When it is appropriate to use slides, ıarts, film, or flip charts at a presentation, be sure you re thoroughly familiar with the contents and have prac-ced exactly how to show-and-tell your way through it. /hen using visual aids, brevity and simplicity work best; ıe purpose is to dramatize and clarify your key points, ot to sidetrack your audience's attention or let him/her ›rget why you are there. For most people, less is more. 'hey don't want to swallow endless charts and numbers; ıey can digest only the essence. It's your job to distill the ıformation for them before you present your material, nd to be prepared to follow up with a précis of how you rrived at the data and how it relates to the points you re making. Spending the time and money to have your ıaterial professionally prepared; sloppy or childish raftsmanship can only work against you. If you're plan-ıing a slide show or film, check out in advance whether he room is equipped with electrical outlets and whatever ound and lighting facilities you'll need, and be certain ıat your own or your rented equipment is in perfect vorking order.

The Stage Set

There are three probable settings for your meeting: at our place, on your prospect's territory, or on neutral round. If the show is to be at your place, give thought to he impression your decor and accessories will make. Are hey reflective of your business and the image you want to convey? Is the space clean and orderly? Is the atmo- phere hospitable, the seating and lighting comfortabl- the appointments convenient? Are you prepared to serv coffee or a meal graciously and efficiently? *Are you in com- mand?*

Renée, a gallery owner, often invites clients into he private office where she can sell them on purchasing ar She orchestrates each meeting from beginning to en starting with the selling environment itself. The walls c her office are hung, sparingly, with excellent examples c the contemporary art her gallery specializes in. The ligh ing is designed to flatter the art and at the same time t make clients comfortable. The background—walls, floo ing, upholstery, and accessories—is done in warm bu muted tones, to produce a quietly cheerful and positiv mood. Renée's office desk isn't a desk at all. Like the re of her office furniture, the desk could be in somebody living room—a gambit that enables clients to visualize th paintings as they would look hung at home. In a cup board, ready for instant use, are an automatic coffe maker, sets of fine-quality china and silver, embroidere linen napkins, and fresh supplies of delectable pastrie The setting Renée has created is rich, tasteful, and env able. It deliberately sets a mood that makes people wan to own what they see.

When you are in the position of choosing a publi place for your meeting, you are limited to what is avai able in the area. Even so, there are options, including res taurants, hospitality suites, and airport conference room Whatever city you're in, you'll find that public places dif fer in their amenities. Choose the best. Look for detail such as a decor that enhances your image, soundproof ing, privacy, good food and service, telephones and an other facilities you may need. Shop around and pla ıead. Go over every minute detail with the functions ıanager well in advance, and then take out extra inırance by checking every detail yourself just before it's me for your meeting.

Develop a Dialogue

> Selling is a very tense situation for me. I'm always anxious, because it's a situation that involves making a positive presentation of myself and I feel very vulnerable. I feel better having some sort of formula to fall back on, something I'm familiar with. I find that if I go over what's going to happen beforehand, it's like having a road map to someplace I've already been and I can navigate the main routes and side streets and detours as they come up.

In addition to your physical presentation and that ıtangible thing, your style, it is essential that you reearse what you want to say at your meeting, so you can ut your points across with the proper impact. It is also ssential that you think through and rehearse what you ıay *not* want to say: the responses you'll have to make to bjections and reactions you wouldn't plan on in an ideal cenario. Expecting the unexpected is a major component f successful selling, and being fully prepared for disgreement is a winning strategic move.

The following chapter contains a sampling of possile scenarios played out and analyzed for you. I urge you ɔ study the scripts, adapt them to fit your own business r profession, and play them out with a partner, to get ıto the swing of formulating your own. With your uddy, go over the questions you will ask in order to get s much information as you can about your prospect's ıeeds and situation before you start selling. Line up the high points of your product or service and strategize ho best to present them. Have your partner talk back to yo so you can respond with appropriate dialogue. Have h play the devil's advocate and give you arguments and o jections, then practice ways you can respond that will co vince her to agree with you. Try closing the deal. T negotiating the terms of your sale. Try several differe scripts, and after each run-through get feedback from you partner and analyze what has happened. What did yo do well, where did you go wrong, how could you impro your performance? Replay the scene with the suggeste improvements and see how it goes. Go through eac scenario from opening small talk to closing, then swit roles with your partner, so you can get inside your pro pect's character and understand his or her reactions. Pl the dialogue out fully, so you'll be comfortable as well a prepared.

Reality: *In selling, everything is possible when you kno what you're doing before you do it.*

The Applause You Hear May Be Your Own

Selling is its own reward. The joy of persuading peop and the satisfaction of accomplishing what you set out t do cannot be matched. They can be augmented, howeve by material rewards you give yourself; rewards that ar incentives for completing what may be difficult for yo and that provide the recognition you need and deserve.

Preplan your reward. If it's a big sale you're aft and you make it, give yourself a big present as a bonu Redecorate a room, take a trip, buy a new coat. If you complishment is smaller—just setting up and getting rough a presentation, for example—give yourself a naller gift: a manicure, a taxi ride, a self-indulgent scrap lingerie. The point is to acknowledge that you've succeeded in completing a cycle, and to establish one more lid reason for setting and completing goals.

Reality: *You are the only headliner you have. Make the ost of your chances.*

12

The Anatomy of a Sale

I think selling is really convincing someone of the impo tance of something to them. It could be anything, an al stract idea. You have to first be knowledgeable and se ond, be aware of the benefits of whatever you're trying t sell to the other person.

Just as there are many types of sales, there are man variations in the selling process and no single script ca apply to all the different situations you'll encounter. Ye the basics of the selling process are always the same: Yo open, you explore for information, you meet objection you negotiate, and you close. One of these phases may b brief, another lengthy; each stage will vary with each sal Their sequence may be shuffled around and some ma not enter into certain pitches at all.

What follows is an overview of the facts of makin presentations: the anatomy of selling. The scenes an mmentary here are guidelines, not formulae, for there is formula for making a sale. In this chapter we will plore and analyze the dynamics of several different sit-tions, so you can adapt the theories and techniques to rious selling needs by shifting the elements of timing, quence, emphasis, and style as situations dictate.

nario I. The anatomy of a sale from opening to closing.

st. Jenny Hanson. Account executive for a New York public relations agency. Her goal: to sell a new and sophisticated financial marketing concept to a midwestern corporation. She is wearing a fashionably tailored suit and blouse. The look is professional and business-oriented; Jenny is there to make a sale, not to socialize.

Prospect. Senior management team of Fortune 500 company.
President: warm, pleasant; wears $450 Brooks Brothers suit.
V.P. Finance: pleasant but distant; dressed in brown plaid suit with vest.
Public relations director: suave, charming, tries to put everyone at ease.

tting. The president's office: Persian rugs, brown leather sofa, ahogany bookcases. Office and executives' clothing say "very nservative, very masculine."

Jenny:	[*Just before meeting, she yawns deeply and says to herself*] Be organized. Compose yourself. This is good for them. You are going to aid them, so you shouldn't be concerned. You are offering a service	Yawning relaxes her tense muscles, giving herself a pep talk reduces tension about going into a situation that is new to

	that's going to be marvelous for them, so it's to their benefit that you are here.	her, to sell concept new to prospect.
Jenny:	I'm pleased to meet you. I'm Jenny Hanson. Thank you for the coffee.	
President:	Did you have a good flight in?	
Jenny:	Very pleasant and right on time. And it's such a nice day. Well, actually, it isn't, is it? It seems to me it's always cold when I'm in Chicago. Do you ever have good weather?	*Opening* small talk. Friendly. Nonsubjective. Topics they can all agree on. Relaxes tensions, establishes human connection.
V.P.:	[*Laughter*] We do have good weather from time to time.	
Jenny:	I think it would be of great assistance, as I mentioned to Jim, your PR director, and of great importance for your company to participate in this year's international investors' conference. This is our second conference and we had a great number of Europeans express interest in your company last year at our West Coast meetings. As I mentioned in my letter to you, we are expecting between forty and fifty European institutional investors this year, basically the portfolio managers and decision-makers.	Makes *transition* from small talk quickly, once tensions are relaxed. *Pitch* states why she is there; points out features of what she is selling; opens discussion to questions/objections that will tell Jenny more about company's areas of need.

President:	Why do you think that's going to be of assistance to us?	Interest aroused; wants to know more.
Jenny:	You have a great deal of outstanding stock, Europeans are very interested in your company, and this is an excellent opportunity to put those two facts together.	Immediately answers with *benefit* to company. Shows she has done *research* and knows her business.
V.P.:	Why isn't it better for us to go to Europe on our own than to meet with a group of Europeans here?	Mild *objection.*
Jenny:	First, by going to Europe, you'll be taking manpower away from your office. The three of you, as the senior management team, would have to go. Second, you can only hit ten institutions at the most in a week's time; ten, if you keep really busy. And they're not all going to be able to see you.	She has thought through this objection and her answer beforehand, during *rehearsal.*
	By attending the conference instead, in the space of an hour and a half you can speak before forty to fifty key investors who represent nine different countries.	*Blends* objection with strong *benefit.*
	You couldn't possibly do that in a week in Europe, could you?	Poses question that will get *agreement.*
President:	You're right. You have a very fine concept.	Gets *agreement.*
	But I would feel awkward paying a PR firm $4,000 for one and a	*Objection* to cost.

	half hours of these Europeans. It's as if I'm buying their attention.	Shows conservatism.
Jenny:	Quite the contrary. You and nineteen other companies will be paying the Europeans' expenses with that $4,000. And that cost includes the fee for our public relations firm.	*Handles objection* by justifying and diminishing cost.
President:	I see. That sounds like a good idea.	*Agreement.*
Jenny:	Yes, I think this would be extremely worthwhile for you. You know, the $4,000 for the hour and a half with your key prospects is the same as three first-class tickets to Europe that would take your key people out of the office for a week.	*Supports* agreement and reinforces *benefit* of cost efficiency.
V.P.:	I must say I'm somewhat leery. You've only held one of these conferences before. Are these the decision-makers who attend? What other companies have signed up on this?	*Objection* shows he needs credentials and endorsement.
Jenny:	The ABC and XYZ companies have both signed up. They're both Fortune 500 companies, also, as you know. There are others, but it's premature to mention them. But you are in good company, I assure you. Here is the list of corporations that	*Supports* need by providing *validation.*

	participated last year, major corporations and financial institutions. They found it a very successful venture. I'll leave these brochures and letters with you, if I may.	Came *prepared* with documentary validation. *Proof* of performance. *Leave-behind* pieces.
V.P.:	I do think it's a good idea, and we would like to participate. Could you tell us a bit more about your PR firm?	*Agreement* and *interest.* Still needs *validation.*
Jenny:	Here is some literature you may keep. It has a list of our clients, tells what we do for them, and there are some reprints of news items on us as well. Now, it's fortunate that I'm here at this time because we still have one of the first-of-the-week slots open for your presentation, and it would be to your advantage to choose an afternoon slot starting at four o'clock so you could move right into a reception and dinner that you can sponsor. That way you'll get extra time to talk with the European investors.	Came *prepared* to document her firm's credentials with leave-behind pieces. Having heard *interest* moves immediately into *trial close.* Takes *risk* of losing the sale by *limiting choice* to time company may not be able to use. *Extends* sale by adding benefit of sponsoring meals PR firm would otherwise have to pay for.
President:	That's a very good idea. What kind of money would that run into?	
Jenny:	That would be perhaps $500 at the most. However, with that additional time, you can get into social conversation and create personal rapport,	*Justifies* cost by turning it into a strong *benefit.*

	which you can't really do in the hour and a half you'll be speaking from the podium.	
V.P.:	Your propositions sound very good. We want to think about it.	*"Maybe."*
Jenny:	Fine. Why don't I give you a call this Friday for your answer. Meanwhile, if any questions come up, please call me.	Puts a *time limit on Maybe* and *asks for decision,* while allowing time for company to check on PR firm's credentials.
	Thank you very much for taking time out of your day to see me. I appreciate it very much.	*Ends* meeting, knowing *strong interest* has been expressed.

Follow-up. Jenny keeps in touch during the forty-eight hours by sending individual thank-you letters to the three principals, restating her proposition and the benefits she can provide for them:

"I thoroughly enjoyed meeting with you last week regarding the international investors' conference.	Restates purpose.
I do hope you and your associates will be able to make the presentation of your company's background and growth potential.	Adds idea.
I know from our surveys that Europeans are interested in your company. At this time we have tentatively slotted you into Thursday, November 4 at 4 P.M., and I	Supports benefit.

	will be in touch with your office to discuss the logistics of your presentation. Thank you again. Cordially, Jenny Hanson"	Assumes Yes decision.

Closing. Jenny relates how she closed the sale: "Forty-eight hours later, I called the president. I prefer going to the top because that's where the ultimate decision is made, and I would much rather try to talk him out of a No than talk other people into rediscussing it with him. He said, 'We'd like very much to participate. Please be in touch with our vice-president of finance, who will be handling all the arrangements.' We wrote a contract on our firm's letterhead stating that the company had agreed to make a presentation on November 4 at four o'clock at a fee of $4,000, half of which would be paid sixty days prior to the conference, with the balance coming due thirty days after the conference. The contract also stated that the company would sponsor a reception and dinner, and that my PR firm would be available to assist them in all the logistics. It was a win/win sale."

Scenario II. (The following illustrates one of the many possible variations on this sales presentation. The cast, setting, and situation are the same as in Scenario I.)

Jenny:	I'm pleased to meet you. I'm Jenny Hanson. Thank you for the coffee.	
President:	Did you have a good flight in?	
Jenny:	Very pleasant and right on time. And it's such a nice day. Well, actually, it isn't, is it? It seems to me it's always cold when I'm in Chicago. Do you ever have good weather?	*Opening* small talk. Friendly. Nonsubjective. Topics they can all agree on. Relaxes tensions, establishes human connection.

V.P.:	[*Laughter*] We do have good weather from time to time.	
Jenny:	I think it would be of great assistance, as I mentioned to Jim, your PR director, and of great importance for your company to participate in this year's international investors' conference. This is our second conference and we had a great number of Europeans express interest in your company last year at our West Coast meetings. As I mentioned in my letter to you, we are expecting between forty and fifty European institutional investors this year, basically the portfolio managers and decision-makers.	Makes *transition* from small talk quickly, once tensions are relaxed. *Pitch* states why she is there; points out features of what she is selling; opens discussion to questions/objections that will tell Jenny more about the company's areas of need.
President:	We're not even in *The Wall Street Journal*'s stock exchange listings, so why do you think this will be of importance to us?	*Objection* that provides *information.*
Jenny:	I beg to differ with you. You are most definitely included in the New York Stock Exchange listing that appears in the eastern edition of the *Journal.* If you'll excuse me a moment, I'll call my office and we can check it out right away . . . . Yes, here are the quotations on your stock at yesterday's closing.	*Makes client wrong.* She could have said, "Of course, not living in the East you don't get a chance to see that edition of the *Journal.*" Points out that she did not offer an incorrect *fact.*
President:	Isn't that interesting. Do all	*Informs* her that

	our releases to Dow Jones go into *The Wall Street Journal?*	president is inexperienced in area of public relations. Provides helpful information, but fails to *control agenda* and stay on *goal.*
Jenny:	Well, of course they pick up all your dividend releases. If it's a story about new appointments in senior management, sometimes it'll be picked up and sometimes not. It depends on if your story is as important to the writer as some other story that's breaking.	
PR Dir.:	As a matter of fact, she's right, Mr. Jones. That's the way it operates.	
Jenny:	Oh yes, these are the kind of things we do for our clients all the time: placing articles in *The Wall Street Journal.* Are you expecting a management change soon?	Strays further from *agenda* and begins to sell PR instead of investor's conference.
President:	No. Of course, that would be very hush-hush information, anyway.	Does not express *confidence* in Jenny.
Jenny:	Our main job is investor relations and we specialize in placing stories and interviews with financial publications to improve the image of our clients' companies or to make stockholders or potential investors interested in purchasing stock.	Has lost the *agenda.*
President:	That's very interesting. I didn't realize there are companies that specialize in that.	
Jenny:	Yes, sir. We represent a	

	number of major corporations for just that purpose. Here is a list of our clients. But that's why I'm here today, to discuss your corporation and the European interest in it.	Tries to return to her *purpose* and revive interest in proposal.
President:	We aren't too eager to have our stock going out to Europeans.	*Objection* that opens opportunity to *explore* for information.
Jenny:	Can you tell me why?	*Asks* for *information.*
President:	Well, we're a midwestern company and we like to have midwesterners owning our stock.	Conservative. Jenny is in the wrong place. Should have determined *attitude* and *interest* before making call. She wasted her time by failing to do *research,* which would have told her that this company will require two to three years *education* before she can sell an innovative concept to them.
President:	You do have an interesting idea, though. May I have your card, and we'll be in touch with you.	"*Maybe.*" Very disinterested. Jenny will have to initiate any further contact.
Jenny:	Just a minute. It must be in here someplace. There's my hairbrush. Oh, and my	Loses *control* by being disorganized. Loses any

makeup. Wait a minute; it's here someplace. I'll find it. Just let me put these things on your desk, if you don't mind.	possible image of professionalism.

Opening a Meeting

The technique of *opening* a meeting is to use small talk in order to establish rapport based on honesty that will open the lines of communication and begin to build agreement. Use a base of reality. Begin by finding something in the office that you truly admire, something that will put yourself and your prospect in accord. For example: "What a beautiful view from your office. I love the sight of hills in the background, don't you?" (The reaction: Of course I do or I wouldn't have selected this office. I'm proud of it, too. She's nice; we share the same sensibilities.) "Your collection of books on botany is marvelous. Do you grow plants yourself?" (Now you can talk about your prospect's pet interest.) Or, "What a sparkling smile on that child in the snapshot. How old is she?" What you've selected to open up communications is something you genuinely admire and your comment is absolutely true for you. You've begun on an utterly honest note that sets the tone for credibility and commonality as you go along. Later, as instinct directs, you'll be able to bolster that rapport from time to time with truly felt compliments on the person's actions as well as possessions. You might say, for example, "I admire your enthusiasm." Or, "You're so clear on your needs." (The implication is that the two of you agree on style, taste, behavior, and probably the product or service you offer, too.)

In your opening, as in every other communication

you ever have with a prospect, always remember this inflexible rule: *Never make the other person wrong.* Your aim is to get agreement, not argument; to do business, not battle; and the minute you make a prospect feel stupid, insulted, or inadequate, he or she is going to turn negative. There are simple and effective techniques by which you can acknowledge a person's error or difference of opinion without making him or her wrong. Phrases that turn the trick are:

- *That's a good point.* Let me add that in my experience many people have quite different reactions to our product.
- *I can see why that's an important thing for you to know.* Our deliveries are sometimes slow, and I'd like to explain how the system works.
- *Many people feel as you do initially,* but after using our services they usually feel quite the opposite.
- *It's interesting that you bring that up.* I felt the same way at first, until my company ran a survey with results that surprised us all.

Making Timing Work for You

Your opening may be brief, as Jenny's was, or it may go on for twenty minutes or so if you divine that your prospect is a chatty type and there is time for the amenities. Either way, be sure that *you* control the agenda.

There is something else to bear in mind about timing. It varies from region to region. In New York and other urban centers you're going to be given almost no time whatsoever for your entire presentation, from open to close. In other parts of the country, the pace is more leisurely and hospitable. The New Yorker's three minutes becomes twenty, thirty, forty minutes in the South, West, and midsections of the country. You'll want to match the prevailing tempo so you fit in agreeably, but you'll also need to protect yourself. Drawling charm and courtesy are delightful, but they can be costly when your time is worth money and you're geared to a fast track.

The best advice, if you need to nudge a meeting along, is to *handle with care.* Move the conversation gently on to where you want it to go, in a way that doesn't display impatience or make the other person feel he or she is wrong. On the other hand, if you find yourself being rushed into a jet-speed New York orbit, don't despair or feel insulted. You can still make all the points you've rehearsed clearly and effectively, minus frills and curtsies.

Creating the Right Mood

Your style should set the mood of confidence. Make direct eye contact with the person you're addressing. Don't stare him or her down discomfitingly, but look directly at the person to whom you're talking; nobody wants to do business with a shifty-eyed salesperson. Keep your body relaxed and open, and avoid nervous body language, the tics and jerky movements that distract attention from your message. Set the tone for your meeting by being enthusiastic. Not necessarily the bubbling-over kind, but enthusiasm that's in keeping with your natural style, that bespeaks your positive outlook, that says, "I feel good about being here." Check your own ego at the door and let the other person do the talking if he or she is a talker. Support everything he or she says; don't try to one-up or make the other person feel wrong.

Observe the courtesies of introductions and name usage. In the same way that youngsters can't be sure which fork to use at their first formal dinner parties, office etiquette can bewilder women who are unaccustomed to business situations. The opening conventions are these:

- Introduce yourself to the secretary and to the people with whom you're meeting by giving both your first and your last names: "I'm Jenny Hanson." Add your company affiliation and position if the information is relevant or necessary.
- In the reception room, tell the secretary your name and provide the information that you have an appointment with So-and-So at such-and-such a time. Give her your card to make it easy for her to copy down your name.
- Unless you are asked to do otherwise, address people considerably older than yourself by their surnames: Mr. Jones; Miss, Mrs. or Ms. Smith. When in doubt as to title, ask the secretary how your prospect likes to be addressed.
- Be alert to the conventions in generally informal companies such as advertising agencies and publishing houses, where the use of first names is usually preferred.
- Shake hands with everyone on entering and on leaving a meeting. Initiate the action yourself. You're not playing Scarlett O'Hara; you're an assured professional woman.
- Give your business card to each person at the meeting, at the outset or as you leave, depending on the situation.
- Be generous with your thank-you's, and be sure to

include recognition of the secretary who serves you coffee or provides other amenities.

Maintain an atmosphere that is courteous and friendly, but be certain you stay in control of the agenda so that you can get your message heard. Remember that whoever holds the agenda is in the seat of power, because that is the person who can include or exclude topics from the conversation. When things begin to get out of hand, as they are apt to do, you can stay in control by using the technique of the Three A's: Acknowledgment, Agreement, and Agenda-control.

Here is a common situaiton the Three A's can rescue you from. You are sitting in your prospect's office and he or she is distracted. There's a look of boredom, or impatience, or of being mentally out to lunch. The phone rings ceaselessly, secretaries run in and out, and your prospect is paying little attention to you. Instead of feeling you've invited disapproval, launch into the Three A's. Start by *acknowledging* what is happening. Say, "You seem to be having an extremely busy day." Then get *agreement:* "I'm sure you'd like to complete what it is that's going on in your office." Having given your prospect the opportunity to complete his or her cycle, go on to regain control of the *agenda:* "I'd like to present my story so you can understand it completely. It'll only take ten minutes to tell you about what I have for you; would you like to take that ten minutes now? Or would you rather complete the other things you're working on and I'll wait outside for a few minutes and come back when you're done?" Then, when your prospect has chosen between the two reasonable and considerate options you've presented, you can go on with your message, sticking to the ten-minute limit you promised and staying in control of the agenda.

Moving into the Sales Pitch

Make the transition from opening to pitch as soon as you feel that rapport has been established and tensions are relaxed. You may say something as simple as, "Let's get to the business at hand" or "Let me tell you why I'm here" to move the discussion forward. Or you might make the transition by using a piece of information you have that relates to the client's or customer's affairs and eases you into business talk: "I've been reading in the papers about the difficulties your industry has been having with strikes. I ran into our mutual friend, John Jones, yesterday, and he says you've had to cut back on production this quarter because of it." In this example, using a mutual contact's name adds further to your credibility.

The sales pitch usually begins with your stating or restating the reason for your meeting, and succinctly stresses benefits to your prospect. Beginners are apt to throw all fifty-two of their cards on the table at this point, a sure way of confusing a customer and making no sales point at all. You should start by playing only your ace instead, describing the one major benefit your product or service offers to your prospect, the one card that will capture his or her interest.

For example, you're meeting with a candy manufacturer and from information you've gleaned through newspaper items or inside gossip, prior research has informed you that your prospect's major problem is the increasing cost of ingredients. Selecting the part of your company's service that fits into the problem, you lead off with the benefit you can provide: "I'm aware that you are having a great deal of trouble because of costs, Mr. Sweet. Our company has devised a system by which you can test whether using less sugar in your candies will produce a product with customer-appeal. Let me add that the idea of a candy with low sugar content will give you a big promotional advantage: Your ads can stress the healthy, natural-food approach."

Having captured your prospect's interest with something that will benefit him or her, you can then move on into a brief visual or oral presentation that explains the features of the benefit. This should take no more than three or four minutes, at which time you can move into exploring for information about your prospect's needs, if you are not already fully informed.

Exploring for Information

If you have thoroughly rehearsed the exploratory dialogue and its possible variations, you already have some idea of what you want in terms of information. Don't worry about it if you forget half your rehearsed lines. You will still get the information you need and make the points you want to make if you are well prepared.

Your aim in *exploring* is to discover what the other person needs so you can offer to help. You should come to each meeting with a prepared list of questions to ask, just as a reporter gets information with the Who-What-Where-When-Why formula. Here is a generalized list of questions you might ask:

- What are you doing now?
- How would you like to change?
- When would it be possible to change?
- Under what circumstances would you consider changing?
- What other considerations would you have?

More specifically, the situation might call for questions such as "What is the average salary of your employees? What is the average turnover per year? What is your peak production season? In which month do you ship? In which period are your profits lowest?" When you have completed your questioning, you will have heard the answers from the other person. You won't be rushing to assumptions and he or she will have to stand or expand on what's been said.

Exploring for Clarification

Really listen to the answers to your questions, and to what the other person is trying to say and is really saying. Play back the responses to be sure you understand each point clearly, and to evoke more information. One effective way of doing this is to repeat the last words you hear as a question. It's what psychiatrists do all the time—at fifty dollars an hour, thank you very much. The client says, "We have a shipping room situation that demands continuous rescheduling," and you respond, "Your shipping room demands continuous rescheduling?" The reply to that will probably supply information, such as, "That's right. You see, orders for our goods come in batches that are sometimes large, sometimes small. What we need is a system that will help us keep track of the work flow so we're not wasting downtime."

Then you could move in with a direct offer: "So you're not wasting downtime? I see. I could set up a series of interviews with your people and analyze just where the waste can be absorbed profitably, then recommend to you certain charts that would let you track your scheduling consistently."

Here is a sample exploring script, complete with played-back questions:

Q: Why do you prefer brand X?
A: Habit, I guess. We always had brand X at home when I was a child, so I just continue to use it.
Q: Habit?
A: Well, I did try other brands, but I always came back to brand X.
Q: I see. You have tried other brands?
A: Yes, but they always seemed to lack that special something that brand X has.
Q: Tell me more.
A: Well, for one thing brand X has just the right amount of sugar in it. It has a flavor the whole family likes. We never had a competing brand that everyone wanted to eat. I might like the sweetness of another one better, and the kids wouldn't. So I figured, why hassle the family? If everyone is going to eat X, why keep trying others out on them? Especially since the others are more expensive.
Q: More expensive?
A: At least a nickel a package more.
Q: Do you have any other reasons for preferring brand X?
A: No. Just habit.

Other exploring phrases to use are: Can you explain more? What else? In what way? I'm not sure I understand, tell me more. I see, and then what?

You can also get information from specific questions such as these: Do you have something particular in mind? What kinds of clothes do you feel comfortable in? How do you feel in the dress you're wearing today? What was the best outfit you bought in the last two years; what was good about it?

Highlights of Exploring

Whether you are selling a product, a service, or yourself, the process is the same:

- Pinpoint your client's important needs by asking questions.
- Sell to those needs by presenting benefits.
- Assume nothing.
- Stick to your agenda.
- Inspire confidence.
- Get agreement all along the way.
- Summarize each segment as you go along.
- Say what you have to say pleasantly and with conviction.

Getting Information from Someone Who Won't Talk

Sometimes you meet a prospect who just won't respond to your probing. One way to get the information you need is to limit the questions to those requiring a Yes or No answer, such as: Do you want a loose or formfitting dress? Do you like brand X better than the other brands? Is scheduling shipments a problem? Do you like natural cereals?

Exploring to Find the Hot Button

In the process of drawing out problems, you're going to find out what your prospect's greatest need is, the biggest desire, his or her hot button. Whether it's price, status, practicality, or something else, you want to hit that hot button—sell to your prospect's need—fulfill his or her desire by offering a benefit. In the following example, validation is added to the benefit of cost savings: "I can see what your problem is and why you're wary about investing in any more equipment at this time. You know, the ABC Company had a problem very similar to yours. They tried our system and it not only straightened out the problem, ABC found its profits rose by 12 percent in the first year. And the investment in our equipment had paid for itself within the first six months."

Reality: *Ask and you shall receive. Explore and you shall find.*

The Trial Close: The Biggest Exploration of All

As early as possible during your exploratory phase, the minute you get agreement on the points you have presented and your prospect shows interest, test the waters to find out whether the person you are speaking with actually has the authority to finalize the sale. This is the trial close, and it is the ultimate probe. What you are doing is finding out if you are in the right place and whether you should continue with your presentation or move on to somebody else. Clarifying your position through a trial close can save you an enormous amount of time, even though it is a risk that many people back away from taking.

A trial close can reveal vital information for you to work with. For example, early in your exploration, you might say, "It sounds as if you think these books are just right for your curriculum. I think an order of two hundred would be just right." Then, if your prospect counters with something like, "Two hundred books! What are you talking about? Ten is as many as we can possibly use," you have received information as to what's considered a reasonable quantity. You've also confirmed that your prospect is definitely interested in your books.

You test the waters with, "A hundred-thousand-dollar contract with us sounds like what your company needs," and you get back this valuable information: "A hundred thousand dollars! That's madness; the most we ever spend is five thousand." Now you know what ball park you're playing in.

You trial-close by asking for your prospect's signature on a contract and you hear, "Sign the contract! I'm in no position to sign contracts around here. You'll have to go to management with that." Wonderful! You've learned where the power really is. Go back and explore what slant the *two* of you should take for a meeting with the decision-makers.

Reality: *It's scary to take risks; you have a chance of losing. Take* educated *risks.*

Handling Objections

Everybody is not going to agree with everything you propose. But disagreement or objection doesn't necessarily mean you've lost a sale. It means the other person has been listening to you, and that's a positive sign; it's an opportunity to go ahead and find out how you can win the sale.

Bear in mind that there are two kinds of objections: real ones and those based on personal opinion. Real objections are based on fact such as, "Your prices are not competitive," "You lack experience and validation, so I cannot use you," "We have had real problems with deliveries by your company."

A real objection requires an immediate answer or your sale will be stopped in its tracks. Most often it will be an objection you've heard before and anticipate hearing again, so you will have come to a meeting armed with refutation: documents, letters of recommendation, ad reprints. Then, when the objection arises, you'll be prepared with an answer: "Yes, you've made a really good point. Another of our clients had the same problem and we solved it very well. Let me show you the letter he sent me afterward." Or, "Yes, I've heard that said before. Another client had the same initial impression you've just stated. He decided, even though he objected to the same point, to try our services on a trial basis. Here's a letter he wrote afterward telling how pleased he was. What had seemed like a problem to him turned out to be a very positive feature, as you can see by what he said."

Another good way to overcome a real objection immediately so as not to lose the sale is to take immediate action, such as calling your office on the spot and making an arrangement that will satisfy your client or customer. "You're quite right; our shipments to you last season were not on schedule. If I may use your phone, I'll call our warehouse expediter right away and ask him to set up priority shipping for you."

A real objection has the further advantage of identifying a problem for you, thus enabling you to come up with the solution. Perhaps the objection is to price. You can shift the focus by slicing your cost into digestible portions. Let's say you're selling a service that costs $500 and the customer says, "That's way too much money; I'm just a small business." You can make the $500 easier to cope with by dividing it into realistic bits: "Yes, and $500 for a whole year comes to less than $10 a week. That's not very much money for the service you'll be getting."

The second kind of objection, that based on personal opinion, deserves short shrift. Minimize it and get on to what's really important in your presentation. Off-the-wall objections can't be answered by documentation, and they're not substantive enough to stop your sale, so play them down. You can get past objections such as "I don't like red and I wouldn't have it in my store," and on with the flow of your presentation quite easily with answers such as "Yes, we all have personal preferences. I don't like red either." Or, "I'll be covering that point in just a few minutes."

For every negative or iffy reply, you'll find there's a question you can ask that will reveal areas of need not yet uncovered, needs that you may be able to fill. Begin by playing back each objection so you'll find the need, as in these examples:

Q: You say your budget is too tight at this time? Is that your main objection or is there something else that bothers you?	You're looking for another problem, one that you can help with.
Q: If I understand you correctly, you already have a data system. Does it include a memory capability?	You're finding a benefit your competitor cannot offer.
Q: I know how you feel when you say you don't really want this system because it would add procedural steps and be bothersome. Actually, my company will work out all the preliminaries and take care of the execution of them as well. So you see, your people won't have to become involved.	You're getting rid of that objection and at the same time opening a door so your prospect can voice another need.

Q: You're correct, we do charge more than similar companies; 10 percent more, in fact. We also deliver weekly rather than monthly and have a record of absolute reliability, as these letters show. Of course there's a price tag on that kind of service. Isn't it important to you to have your deadlines met quickly and consistently?

You're confronting the objection with absolute honesty, minimizing it and isolating the competitive advantage you can provide, and presenting proof of your claim.

Here is another example of one way to meet objections. The scenario also illustrates how to blend customer needs with product or service features and benefits.

In this scenario, Ina, an educational materials sales representative, is about to make a sales pitch to the representatives of a remedial reading department of a school. They are Jane, the director, and Ralph, her assistant. The setting is the director's office.

The opening, transition, and initial pitch have taken place. There has been a discussion of the department's needs for the school year, and Ina has shown samples of her product, a new remedial reading book series. Her goal is to sell three hundred of these kits to the school.

Ina: This is our new remedial reading kit. I know that in the lab you're talking about, your students read on about a fourth-grade level. This kit is written on a second- to fourth-grade reading level and would be very appropriate for your students. It would meet the goals

Plays back and *summarizes* prospect's needs; *blends* product *features* and *benefits* with department's *needs.*

	you've mentioned: comprehension, finding the main idea and character development. Its content consists mostly of short stories, ideal for students like yours whose attention span is short.	
Jane:	You know, I hate these books. They're not good literature. Why are we giving the kids such junk?	*Objection.*
Ina:		Ina is silent, knowing Ralph will intervene on behalf of his own interest. He does, and makes a *selling point.*
Ralph:	These kids are not going to read good literature. This junk is all they want because it relates to them. It uses the kind of language and characters they can understand.	
Ina:	Yes, that's right.	*Supports* prospect's statement.
Jane:	The paper it's printed on is terrible. Not only does it yellow right away, you can see through the other side.	Valid *objection.*
Ina:	That may very well be the case and the reason it's printed on this kind of paper is so we can sell it at such a low price. If it were on better paper, it would cost too much and you wouldn't be able to use it at all.	*Honest* response. *Blends objection* to poor quality with advantageous *feature.*
	Not only that, this isn't a basic reading series. It's designed to grab the interest of the slow learners, who aren't known for treating their books with any care. We put our money into grabbing the kids' attention.	Adds a *benefit.*

	That's what you really want, isn't it?	Seeks *agreement.*
Ralph:	That's exactly what we want.	*Agreement.*
Ina:	So it doesn't really matter about the paper, does it?	*Summarizes* for *agreement.*
Jane:	Well, no, but I would prefer better paper.	Objection diminished.
Ina:	I agree with you. I'd prefer it, too, but this is what we have for the price, and it is the kind of reading material you need.	*Makes customer right* and *shares taste* in quality. *Reinforces* selling rationale.
Jane:	That makes sense. If the kids like this kind of book, it will develop their reading skills and increase their interest in reading other books.	*Objection* overcome. Prospect mentions *benefit.*
Ina:	So these really meet your needs, don't they? If we put one kit into each school, it comes to about $20,000.	*Confirms* product's *advantages* to school reading department. Begins *trial close* by *exploring* budget capability.
Ralph:	Oh my! We only have a $30,000 budget. How can we spend two thirds of the budget on these books!	*Objection* to price.
Ina:	Well, you need these kits and you need one for every lab, so you need to buy the whole series. There's nothing else around that you can get for this kind of price.	*Overcoming objection* by restating prospect's *need* and *limiting their options.*
Jane:	I wish we had the money for it.	Expresses *desire.*
Ina:	If you take the kits, I can get you some additional kits from another reading level at no cost—enough to fill the needs of twenty more schools.	*Adds to advantage* of buying the kits by offering to *fill additional need at no cost.*

Jane:	That would be ideal.	The turning point of the sale has been reached.
Ina:	We can put one in every lab, then. Do you want me to send the kits out now? Can you get me a purchase order?	*Closes* in on their interest. *Limits choice to* "when," not "Yes or No."
Jane:	Now wait, I don't have the money yet.	
Ralph:	I have some money. We could split the billing between our budgets; we buy the same materials anyway.	Customer finds a way.
Ina:	Why don't I send the whole order of three hundred kits. Ralph can pay his share now, and we'll delay the rest of the billing until your money comes in, Jane.	*Begins closing* sale by negotiating agreeable payment schedule, rather than waiting for total budget and probably losing total sale.
Jane:	That would be fine. But Lorna isn't here to type up the purchase order now.	
Ina:	Tell you what. You give me a purchase order and I'll sit down and type it up. And I'll walk it through the board for you as well, so you can have the first half paid for. I'll have the entire shipment to you in three weeks.	*Closes sale* and offers *personal help* in order to expedite conclusion. Finalizes terms of *negotiation* to *close sale.*

Handling Objections When the Product is You

When a job, raise, or promotion is what is on your agenda, the techniques for handling objections are the same as when you are selling a tangible product or another kind of service. Consider how these typical objections are met, for example:

You say your budget is too tight at this time? Is that your main objection, or is there something else that bothers you?	*Explore* to find other *needs you can fill.* You may learn that your prospect isn't sure you have had enough experience; then you can produce documentary *evidence* that you have.
If I understand you correctly, you already have a good photographer on tap. Can that person also do setups, or do you have to hire a stylist in addition?	*Explore* to find a *competitive advantage* you can offer.
I know how you feel, that you don't really want to hire another photographer because it would add procedural steps and be bothersome. Actually, I have excellent sources for procuring all the equipment I'll need and will take care of it for you. So you see, your purchasing department won't have to become involved.	*Make it easy* for the prospect to buy your service.
You're correct, I do want a bigger raise than you've given your	*Ask* for what you are worth.

other photographers; 10 percent bigger, in fact. I also know how to research each project of yours and have a record of never missing a deadline, as these letters from your clients prove. Of course, there's a price tag on that kind of service. Isn't it important to you to have your research and deadline needs met reliably and consistently?

Back your request with reasons why: the *benefits* you have to offer. Offer *proof*.

Negotiating: Coming to Terms

Once you have gotten the signal that your prospect is interested and agrees that he or she wants your product, service, or yourself, it's time to negotiate the sale. "Negotiating" means establishing the terms: how many, when, at what price, what title you'll have . . . the specific details you'll both need to agree on to conclude the deal.

Negotiation can be a very brief phase involving short, direct, factual questions and answers. It can take longer if you need to overcome additional objections, explore further, and/or come up with alternative solutions.

When negotiating occurs before you have gotten a commitment to buy, the naming of prices and terms limits your prospect's choices and makes it easier for him or her to reach the decision to buy or order. "Should I put you down for a dozen of these?" opens the door to "Yes," or "A half dozen is enough right now," or "I think we can use two dozen."

When there is indecision—"I don't know. A dozen sounds good, but I just don't know"—you can get off the Maybe and move matters along by presenting a choice beween two things: "Can you use one dozen or two?" 'Should I start work here on the first or the fifteenth?" People like to have guidance; presenting clear options provides it.

Negotiating may feel to you like taking an outrageous risk. Don't be afraid of it. And don't be too modest about what you ask for. If you start high—with a large sum, an entire service package rather than a single piece, a whole shipment instead of a minimal order—you can always come down. It doesn't work well the other way around. Once you've presented a low or medium term, it's extremely difficult, in the same presentation, to ask for more.

The direct stimulus of discussing prices, delivery dates, quantities, your title, salary, or pension plan can produce the action you're aiming at. And remember, asking for action is the ultimate goal of a presentation—whether the action is an order or another appointment.

Sometimes negotiating comes directly out of handling objections, as in the following.

Cast. Margo, owner of a telephone dictating company
Doris, prospective purchaser
Setting. Margo's office
Synopsis. Margo's company is only two years old and has just begun to show a profit. Because of other circumstances, she wants to sell the company and has been talking for three months with a potential purchaser, Doris. Doris has been hemming and hawing, stuck in a Maybe routine. Last time they met, Margo put a time limit on the Maybe's, pressing for a Yes or a No, and convinced Doris to agree to investigate by December. At the meeting you will read about, Margo has opened by asking the results of Doris's investigation.

Doris:	I've looked into the potential of your company very	*Objection* because of cost.

	thoroughly, Margo, and in view of the investment that would be required of me at this time, my answer is No. I'm just not in a position to make the expenditure.	
Margo:	What I hear you saying is that in terms of making a large investment at this time, you are not willing to do so. Is that your main objection or is there something else that bothers you?	*Summarizes* for clarification. *Explores* for other problems.
Doris:	You're correct. I'm not in a position to make a large investment right now. I also have some doubts as to how this business will take off.	*Information* about other problems.
Margo:	Is there anything else about it that you object to?	*Assumes nothing; explores* for further information.
Doris:	No, there isn't. You have a splendid organization and a great facility. It's probably just what I want, but right now I don't want to make the investment.	Evidence of *interest* and *desire;* primary objection still stands, with added *information* "right now."
Margo:	When do you feel that you would be willing to make it?	*Plays back* "right now" and *limits answer* to "when," not "if."
Doris:	That would be when I think it's closer to taking off.	Inconclusive; *"Maybe."*
Margo:	Let's see what we have here. It's an ideal situation. Our organization and facility are excellent, and it's probably just	*Summarizes* positive points.

	the kind of business you want. You don't have the money to invest in it right now, but you might in the future. And you're not quite sure how it will operate.	The peg to deal from.
	Let me see if I can come up with an alternate plan, so you can see if it is for you. I'd be willing to have you rent the facility, using my personnel, on a trial basis. If it works out well for you, then we can talk about a financial investment further down the line.	*Offers to help* Doris make a decision by *negotiation* of a compromise solution.
	If it doesn't work out, you will have had a trial balloon and I will have gained something, too. How does that concept feel to you?	Offers deal without cost or risk; sets up *win/win situation. Asks for trial order.*
Doris:	I hadn't considered that. It sounds very good. What kind of rental are we talking about?	Prospect is now actively involved in buying decision.

What Margo did was explore Doris's objections to make them crystalline, and then offer an alternative plan that both women could live with. She changed Maybe and No into a probable Yes, which will be a complete win/win situation. Even if the Maybe remains No, Margo will be in an improved situation. Given a decision that completes the cycle, she will be free to move on to the next prospective buyer. And this discussion has now led to a discussion of terms.

In the scenario that follows, Kate, a financial analyst, and Steven, a bank officer, have agreed that Kate will assist Steven on a special project. She has basically made the sale, but her fee has not yet been discussed—and the sale will not be final until it is.

Kate:	Steven, there is something we haven't gotten around to: my compensation. I am more than happy to assist you on this project, but I think we should agree on terms now, before we get too deeply into the work.	Speaks about money *directly* and *openly,* without apology or nervousness.
Steven:	Of course.	
Kate:	Since I am the expert in this area and we agree I'm the person to help, what do you think would be an appropriate fee?	Establishes her *ability to fill his need* and implies that she is worth a significant fee. Gives him the opportunity to *inform* her of what range he has in mind.
Steven:	Well, I don't have a huge budget, but I do need your help. I think $300 a day on a per diem basis is about right.	Gives *information* about price range.
Kate:	Steven, my regular fee is $600 a day. I estimate this project will take approximately six days of my time, so the total would be $3,600.	Begins *negotiating* process, starting higher than what she will accept, to leave room for discussion and win/win agreement.
Steven:	I'm sorry. We have no intention of paying that much. It's out of the question; we never pay $600 fees. The highest we've ever paid is $500 a day.	*Objection.* Provides solid *information* Kate can work with.

Kate:	My regular fee is $600. However, since $500 is the most you have paid to date and since I know you'll be pleased with my work, I'd be willing to compromise this once at $550, on condition that on my next project for you my fee is the regular $600.	*Negotiates* downward gradually, so she won't conclude deal below her minimum of $500 and setting up bigger fee for future projects.
Steven:	I'm afraid $500 is our absolute tops, Kate, and I don't know that we could ever go up to $600.	He has gone from $300 to $500.
Kate:	All right. Let's do this one at your top figure of $500, and then we can negotiate in good faith when the next project comes around.	She has gotten the $500 she wanted by coming down from $600.
Steven:	That sounds very fair. I'll have a letter of agreement drawn up and it will be on your desk by Tuesday.	They both have what they want. It is a *win/win situation.*

Closing the Sale

At the point when you have aroused definite interest, close the deal. Briefly, confirm where you and your prospect stand by summarizing the points you have agreed on and the important benefits you will provide. Be direct about asking for the order or action you came for, and ask for it with the positive attitude that the sale is yours.

What you're looking for is definite action; you want a Yes or a No. And asking for that action is where most women fall apart. They're afraid to take the risk of hearing No. That doesn't make much sense when you stop and realize that unless you ask for action, all the work you've done so far will be useless. And a No isn't going to kill you; it will complete the cycle for you and at the same time give you the opportunity to ask, "Why 'No'?" and then clarify any possible misinterpretation.

The worst word you can hear is Maybe. If that's what you get when you ask for action, just keep on going until you get a definite Yes or No.

Closing is hard because you're asking for a commitment. The way to make it easier is to come from a positive attitude that of course your prospect will agree with your point of view. Ask for the commitment in a positive way: "When shall I start? If you sign these papers now, I can begin next Monday. I'll have my office prepare the plans and I can get them to you by Wednesday. I'll need your signature to get that into motion. From everything we've spoken about, this sounds like it's my job. You like the approach, you're confident I can help you, all that remains is signing the papers and setting the date for when you'd like me on board."

Here's an illustration of how one sale was closed.

Scene IV. Closing the sale.
Cast. Andrea, a fund-raiser for Ivy University. She is wearing a conservative print dress that is womanly but not sexy, low-key but fashionable. It is a presence her prospect can feel comfortable with.

Ruth, prospective donor, widow of Ivy alumnus
Setting. Ruth's living room
Synopsis. Andrea's goal is a $5,000 donation. She has asked Ruth for $5,000–$7,000 to equip an Ivy gymnasium. Ruth has agreed that equipment is needed but was thinking of donating

$3,000. She is not sure about making a donation at this point and is at the Maybe stage.

Andrea:	I want to tell you how very pleased I am with your enormous enthusiasm for Ivy University. From everything you've said, you see as clearly as we do the need for additional equipment for the gymnasium. I think it would be very appropriate to purchase that equipment in your husband's name and to place a plaque on the storage area dedicating it to him. Let's think about what the plaque should say.	*Summarizes* position. *Benefit* that appeals to prospect's *ego.* Makes it *real* by visualizing appearance of plaque.
Ruth:	I like the idea of having a plaque in my husband's name. I think it should be quite small, with very contemporary lettering.	*Agreement.* Plaque has *reality.*
Andrea:	By small, would you say ten inches, or twelve or sixteen? How do you see it?	Bolstering *reality* and making it difficult for prospect to back off.
Ruth:	I'd like something very small, very discreet. I was thinking of a ten-inch plaque.	
Andrea:	Let's see what it will say, so we'll know if the ten inches will take care of it. We'll write it out. I can see the plaque very fittingly in the East Gym-	*Solidifying* reality. Appeal to emotions.

	nasium, where your husband used to watch basketball.	
Ruth:	You are so right.	
Andrea:	In order to equip that gym properly, it would take $7,000 worth of equipment.	Starts *negotiation* with figure higher than goal.
Ruth:	As I told you, Andrea, $3,000 is what I'm prepared to give.	Is out of *Maybe* and into Yes. Only terms remain for concluding.
Andrea:	That's so. Why don't we pick a figure in between the two. If you put in $5,000, I know of some extra funds that can fill out the rest. And the equipment will still be a gift in your husband's memory. Would you like to give us a check or shall we purchase the equipment and have you billed directly?	Starts to complete *negotiation.* Makes it easy for Ruth to *agree* on $5,000, adds *emotional appeal* to seal the idea. *Limits choice* to two.
Ruth:	Have them bill me direct, please.	The sale is *closed.*
Andrea:	Fine. What I need is your authorization. I'll write up an agreement that you are to fund new equipment for the East Gym in an amount not to exceed $5,000. That sum includes the plaque, of course. Let's write out the wording for the plaque, to be sure the spelling is correct; then you can sign the agreement and we will proceed according to your wishes.	Completes *closing sale,* in writing.

Get It in Writing

Once you have closed a sale, be sure you have the agreement in writing, either a contract or a letter of agreement that incorporates all the terms you have settled on: how, when, where, what the project is, the financial terms, everything you've closed on. Spell out each term clearly, so there will be no unpleasant surprises later on and so that you will have something to refer to should a question or a problem ever arise.

Extending the Sale

You can extend your sales even when you're dealing with what may seem to be a single item. If you're an automobile salesperson, for example, you can add accessories to the car, once you have evoked strong interest and are at the closing stage. "You'll want an FM radio, of course, and how about a tape deck to break up those long trips you take. You really ought to have whitewalls, too; they add such a distinctive look." If you're a boutique salesperson, you'll surely want to extend your dress sales by adding a scarf or belt and other accessories: "They coordinate so beautifully, and these shoes and bag really complete the fashion look you're after."

To extend the sale when you're in a service business and already have sufficient proof-of-performance so you're beyond selling one-shots to build up validation, you can ask for a retainer and offer a package of ongoing work, instead of the single project you've discussed. But you have to *ask.* It's up to you to take the initiative if you're going to extend a sale—even though, as a woman, you're accustomed to the passive position of responding to other people's suggestions instead of instigating the action. That is one of the major differences between men and women: Men are active, while women traditionally are passive. It's also one of the major differences between succeeding and not succeeding in the selling game.

You can take the lead and extend your sale when you're selling yourself, also, although there's a bigger risk involved. Unless you have very strong credentials behind you, you may lose everything you've just won if you ask for the moon. In extending the sale of a service or yourself, be realistic about whether you really are worth more than the competition. And be sure that strong interest in you has been established. Here are two situations to illustrate the point:

Sheila was looking for her very first job. She had excellent credentials—a master's degree and all sorts of recommendations from influential contacts—and was obviously extremely bright. She was inexperienced in the business world, but confident of her ability. A contact had spoken to the vice-president of a small computer firm about Sheila, and an interview was arranged. It went well and the vice-president showed a strong interest in hiring her. He asked what she thought her salary should be and Sheila went for broke, asking sixteen thousand—double the amount she thought somebody just out of college could command. When that was accepted, she quickly tried to extend the sale by asking for stock options. At that point, since she lacked experience, the vice-president backed off from hiring Sheila. She would have done better not to try to extend her sale on her first job, but rather to have waited until she had experience to use in negotiating.

Lillian, on the other hand, has been a free-lance

marketing consultant for fifteen years and has gained recognition for proven excellence in her field. When a large manufacturer asked her to provide a new product survey in test market areas, she told him, "I'm pleased that you have come to me. I do test surveys all the time, and I know that it's one of the minor segments of a problem such as yours. You need to know how to position and market your product, as well. I wouldn't feel right selling you a test survey only and then leaving you out there without the follow-through, in a position of possible failure because you lack complete data. I strongly urge that you hire me on retainer to execute the entire package you need, so your new product will succeed."

At this point the manufacturer could have turned on his heel, adamant in wanting the test survey or nothing. Or he could have bought Lillian's extended idea of a complete marketing package because of her successful track record and outstanding professional expertise. She was gambling, and she won.

One of the most obvious areas for extending sales is the field of cosmetics sales. Here the goal for the salesperson is to sell an entire line and to cement customers to her for sales that repeat and repeat. This scenario provides an excellent illustration of extending a sale.

Scene V. Extending a sale.
Cast. Sara, a cosmetics salesperson
Ms. Brown, customer
Setting. A department store cosmetics counter.
Synopsis. Customer walks slowly to counter, browsing.

Sara:	Hello, my name is Sara. I see you're interested in our new fall shades. Would you like to try on that lipstick?	Introduces self to establish friendly contact. *Explores* customer's inter-

	It's the very newest thing for fall and would be very flattering to your skin tone.	est and urges action. (Opening with "May I help you?" would have gotten a Yes or a No and left no room for probing the customer's interest.)
Ms. Brown:	Oh, I'm just browsing.	
Sara:	Fine. My, isn't it nippy today. Fall is really here, I'm afraid.	Relaxes customer by *small talk* on unrelated subject.
Ms. Brown:	Is this the new shade you advertised?	Customer no longer intimidated by the presence of a fashion authority.
Sara:	Yes, it is. This lipstick is so nice and creamy. Let me try it on you. Can you feel the texture?	Presents *selling feature.* Works to arouse *desire.*
Ms. Brown:	Yes, it is quite creamy.	*Agreement.*
Sara:	And another great thing about it is that it stays on all day. You'll get good wear out of this lipstick. A nice thing to do with it is to wear a lip gloss over it, which gives you a shiny, dewy look.	*Supports* first *selling feature* and adds another. *Extending* the sale.
Ms. Brown:	I don't like lip gloss. It's too gooey.	*Objection.*
Sara:	You can use the lipstick by itself if you'd rather. It does have a nice shine to it because it's creamy. How do you like it?	Customer is always *right.* Reinforces basic *selling point.* *Probing* for problems/needs.

Ms. Brown:	It looks quite nice.	*Interest, desire, agreement.*
Sara:	We also have a blush to coordinate with that shade. It's burgundy and it would really set off the lipstick and your own coloring, too. Let me put it on for you.	Appeal to ego. If she *tries* it, she's more apt to buy it.
Ms. Brown:	It's quite nice.	*Interest, desire, agreement.*
Sara:	How about the matching nail polish. It gives such a finished look.	*Extending* sale. Trying to get customer into using entire line.
Ms. Brown:	I never wear nail polish.	*Objection.*
Sara:	You never wear nail polish? But you have such lovely hands.	Tries to overcome objection by appeal to ego.
Ms. Brown:	I hate nail polish and my husband hates it, too.	*Objection.*
Sara:	I see. Perhaps there is something else you can use today. We have a half-price special on our moisturizer. You can get the $13 size for only $6.50.	*Extending* sale. Appeal to price-saving.
Ms. Brown:	I don't think I need a moisturizer. I have one at home.	*Objection.*
Sara:	You have one at home? Fine. When you finish using it up, do come back and see me because I think you'd be very satisfied with this one. It's wonderful for softening the dry lines on your skin.	Meets objection with *promise of benefit.*
Ms. Brown:	I'll just take the lipstick and blusher today.	Makes *decision. Sale closed.*
Sara:	Thank you. Please do come	Leaves customer

back and see me because we get new shades and products all the time, and if there's ever a problem you have I'll be happy to help you. Here's a card with my name and telephone number.	with feeling of friendship and *support*, plus reason to come back. *Makes it easy* for customer to repeat purchase.

Once you've closed the sale and perhaps extended it, assure your client or customer of your friendship and sincerity, support the wisdom of the decision he or she has made—and leave. You both have other things to do, now that this selling cycle is complete.

***Reality:** We are all successful, some more demonstrably than others.*

13

The Follow-up: how to keep on getting what you want

Being a success at selling is like being a successful lover: You need to keep right on being attentive after the climax has been reached. You cement the relationship by showing courtesy, kindness, and friendship. You nourish the other person's confidence in you and what you can do. You're understanding, you're helpful, you never let him or her forget you. In other words, you keep on selling after the sale has been made, to keep the rapport you've established alive and healthy.

Business as well as personal relationships thrive or wither according to what you put into them. They need fresh ideas, constant support, and communication. Lose touch with a client, a customer, or employer and you're apt to lose hold of the business. It's human nature, and good business, too, to stray to where the fields are greener, the ideas fresher, the support and communication stronger. And clients are only human.

In the last decade women have seen the effects of relaxing too much in a business relationship or taking a relationship for granted. They've learned that things can fall apart when you least expect them to. Just when you least expect it, your boss will resign and you will have to start selling yourself to a new one. Or a job will open and you'll have to shift gears quickly because it's a job you should go after. Or you'll learn when it's too late that another salesperson has usurped your biggest buyer. Nothing ever stays the same in business and a good salesperson should always be alert to approaching change, always planning the next move that will turn change to advantage. *Semper paratus,* as we used to say in the troops.

The Rewards of Following Through

There's a chain of good reasons for continuing to be attentive so people will keep wanting what you've got. One is that by keeping the lines of communication open, you can keep gaining information about the other person's needs—needs that you may be able to fill. For another, by keeping the door open you can build your network of contacts. Some people call this "using the user." It is. Face it, a satisfied customer, client, or employer is the best lead you can have to other new customers, clients, or employers. Allison, a time management expert, says that every one of the eighty new clients she has gotten in the past two years came from her first corporate sale. That company recommended her to its subsidiary divisions, then to friends in other businesses and even to relatives who could use her services. In turn, these friends, relatives, and executives have recommended her to *their* friends, relatives, and colleagues, and you can see how the network has spread. It's the Rule of Three at work. Allison keeps it working by keeping in touch with that first client and all her contacts along the line. Each time she closes a sale, she asks for a contact, and then makes sure to report back on what happened. It's a courtesy that is much appreciated.

So make whatever effort it takes, as long as you know that the payoff is statistically worth your time. Call back, make visits, do favors. Keep expressing your interest in your customer's, client's, or employer's welfare and progress. Memories fade fast; your job is to keep reminders of you both present and pleasant.

Reality: *It takes more time and effort to develop a new client than to hang onto an old one.*

Professional Follow-through

As a professional, you will not only sell well, you will follow up on what you sell. You'll stick to the agreements as stated in your contracts. You'll complete each job, well and without complaint, no matter how many difficulties arise. You'll remember that keeping promises is a legal as well as a personal responsibility and will let your clients or customers know immediately if there are to be problems or delays, so that arrangements can be made to adjust to the changes. You'll perform competently and professionally at all times, so that your clients and customers will always want to continue to do business with you.

Keep Records

Your own memory's probably no better than most people's. The first thing to do after a sales call, whether it's successful or not, is to make notes of just what went on. Write an outline of the information you'll want to remember and go over the details with your career partner. Analyze and evaluate what you did right, where you went wrong, what you might try doing differently next time. Keep your notes on file. They'll be valuable as the months and years—and you—progress.

Leads File

Every job lead and contact you collect deserves a place in your file, so all the relevant data will be available to you when you need it. A system I find extremely useful incorporates the device of cross-filing, very much the way libraries cross-file by book title, author, and subject. My headings, always filed alphabetically, are name, city or geographical area, company name and industry. The notations include when and where we met or made contact, the mutual contact, the subjects we discussed, areas of interest, and personal data such as wife or husband's name and hobbies.

I find the Leads File especially helpful when I travel to another city, Los Angeles for example, to speak or make a sales call. Before I go, I look under Los Angeles to see whom I might call on while I'm there, who the contact is and so on. Of course, the same routine applies when no travel is involved. I strongly suggest that you start now to build your own valuable Leads File.

Reality: *Good prospects never file themselves. They just fade away and are lost.*

Evaluate Yourself: Hold Quarterly Meetings with Your "Board of Directors"

Take a leaf from the successful corporations that operate on a quarterly basis and call a meeting with your "board" every three months at least, to evaluate where you stand and where you should be going. Your board—you and your partner—should make each meeting a command performance, formalized by an agenda that's been written out ahead of time. Areas you'll want to discuss, assess, and establish policy or strategy on may include:

- Projects in progress or completed this quarter
- Prospective projects
- Time sheet and cost analysis
- Handling personality problems
- Strategizing about client needs
- Extending sales
- Evaluating your present job
- Planning for a future job

Schedule plenty of time to explore, evaluate, and resolve the topics on your agenda. Brainstorm with your partner for ways to keep business relationships alive. Set up new goals to carry you through the next three-month period. And when the meeting is over, go out and get to work on those goals.

Reality: *A goal well met is a goal well worked on.*

14

How It Feels to Have What You Want

There are rewards for success, there are prices for success, there are choices we must make as we strive for success. As women, we're just beginning to learn what the rewards, prices, and choices are all about. Among the joys is the wonderful feeling of accomplishment and, with it, the ability and privilege of helping others to succeed. As we grow and achieve, we become role models—mentors for other women who wish to follow where we have led. And through mentoring, we add purpose to our lives. For me, that is the greatest feeling of all.

But there's a trade-off for everything and there are prices to be paid for success. Juggling the roles of homemaker and career woman can mean having to give up long-standing customs and relationships. The changes in life-style may unbalance a marriage, alter one's status in the community, affect the way other people react to a "new" personality. If you're unwilling to accept the prices as well as the rewards, there's one alternative: stay home.

Reality: *Every situation breeds a set of problems. It's a matter of which set of problems you would rather have.*

The Prices of Success

The price of success varies with the individual, but almost no woman's life is left unchanged by her strivings for a career. Sometimes the price feels overwhelming, as this fifty-two-year-old publisher reports:

> I paid for my success. It has cost me two marriages, because one price was working without the support of people close to me. My parents, who are in their seventies, are giving me support now, but they didn't for a long time. They didn't understand what I was working so hard for. My mother would say, "Why are you working so hard? You ought to take care of yourself. You should get married." I did get married, at twenty-two. I followed the program totally and had my children right away. I was miserable. So when I was thirty-one I was divorced, with two young children, and I knew that what I had really wanted to do at eighteen was what I had to do now. But there was no community support at that time. I think women's consciousness is more evolved at this time because women are growing up more open emotionally; they don't have to buy into the cultural traps I did when I was twenty-two. What happens as a result is that we have a kind of power, what Germaine Greer called "sexual politics." And women who feel their own power frighten men, because their power structure is based on keeping somebody down.
>
> There is a terrible price, and I'm living through it

right now. It is so hard. I'm in a whole role reversal with my husband, where I'm virtually the mythological man and Richard is the mythological dependent woman, realizing for the first time that he has to enter into a whole new cultural concept. There is the very real joy of professional satisfaction after years of struggle, and I will never put down the personal joy. But I grew up with the mythology of sharing it with somebody, and now the person I want to share it with is scared by it. Success is costing me my second marriage, but not to pay that price is, I think, a greater price. Because not to pay that price, to play out somebody else's script, is to do your own development a disservice.

Family life is rarely unaffected by a woman's efforts to achieve career success. Sometimes roles must be renegotiated; other times they shift in ways that have not been anticipated.

I have stopped family dinners. I don't pay attention to the house. But oddly enough, my kids give me total support. My husband does not, because he's got his own mythology. I think he is typical of many educated men of today who give lip service to women's rights and equality. Intellectually, they think what we're doing is terrific but down deep, they miss all the nurturing, the total caretaking. It's on a very deep level, and it comes out at the countdown. I guess what they really think is that a nine-to-five job is terrific, but when we're really making it, it's different. I have an ongoing fight with Jack that shows what I mean. He traveled five months in the first year of our marriage and never once was concerned about how I was going to manage my business and the household and all the problems that came up while he was away. Now, if I'm away for one evening, he's furious. He accepts what I do so grudgingly, and resents it. It's taken me a lot of looking in the mirror and saying, "I am not guilty," because if I'm not my friend, nobody's going to be.

Sometimes the price is in coping with other people's reactions to your success. It's interesting that most often it is men who cannot accept a woman's professional development, while other women are delighted rather than envious.

> I cannot tell you the number of men who have made jealous remarks: "Oh, you're going to be so rich—wow." They don't do it to put me down necessarily; they're just uncomfortable when they hear of my success. On the other hand, the women I know—not only my women friends but the women who work with me—are all very excited and happy and saying, "Isn't that terrific!" I just feel sorry for men that they come from that space.

The Wages of Learning to Sell

Salespeople have been the butt of many jokes over the years—so many, in fact, that their image has become tarnished in some circles. And for many women, learning that selling is what business is all about is a rude jolt. Perhaps this is because while women sell themselves every day of their personal lives, their efforts in the business world are contrary to all of their cultural conditioning. For many women, learning to sell involves confronting subconscious motivations, redirecting talents and skills that they have been taught were best left lying partially submerged. The following excerpts describe how many women have successfully come to terms with the necessity of selling themselves, their products, or services—and how they have put their skills and talents to work to get exactly what they want from life in a direct, upfront manner.

Changing Attitudes

I went into the field of sales thinking it was very demeaning. I had no respect for it. I thought it was the lowest of the low, and I was just doing it to get out of education. In the beginning, I loved it, although I couldn't understand why. I thought it was such a trivial, meaningless thing and how could I like it? It went on like that for quite a while, until finally I decided that this ridiculous prejudice had to go. Sales was a perfectly valuable job, exciting and stimulating. Maybe it was the way I was brought up, feeling that being in a profession is the only worthwhile thing, that made me come into sales feeling it was beneath me. Now I'm successful. I've learned to push the issues, to be assertive if somebody demurs, to nail down sales. I've learned that this is the work world and that if I want to succeed, I've got to play it the way it works. I think many women are afraid to be assertive even now. The movement has come far, but women are still often afraid to ask how much money there is in a budget—to ask for a sale.

I had a lot of sleepless nights when I started. I felt that I was giving up too much: Other people were out dating while I was out working. But I really feel I have a purpose, and that's made it worthwhile.

When I was a child I would do anything to get a response. I couldn't have the world take me for what I was. I had to become what the world wanted. It took a lot of growing up to learn that I could just be myself, without pleasing the whole world. I think that being in selling is what made me grow up. You get to deal with a lot of reality when you're selling. You get to know people as they really are behind their masks, and they get to see you as you really are, too. You have to be honest about yourself as well as about what you're selling, and the realization that honesty is OK is one of the best things that has happened in my life.

I talk to myself a lot. I call it making a positive self-presentation, and I imagine, from talking to a number of other women, that I'm not alone in doing this. Because no matter how qualified we are, no matter how many degrees we have, no matter how much experience we have, there's a little voice in there that picks on our weak points and insecurities. For me, it's never feeling that I'm quite good enough; maybe I didn't say the right things; I could have handled that a little differently or done this a bit better. I'm getting out of that now and starting to think, "Well, that's the way it was. Just move on and make it better next time." Turning all those negatives around really has helped my frame of mind. I've also learned that when you're doing my kind of work, you can't please everyone—and you can't take it personally. It's not you they don't like—they don't have time to get to know you, anyway. So you talk to yourself in a very positive way, focusing on all the good things you have, on your strengths. You build on those. Getting it straightened out has given me so much confidence. Instead of thinking, "They don't want me," I think, "Look what I have to offer." For me, that's one of the most important things: self-awareness, being aware of all your strengths and trying to bolster them, taking responsibility for yourself. That's the key ingredient that a lot of people really don't grasp. You are the one in total control of your life. Once you understand that, you can have it all.

I had to work my way through the ego part of competing with other salespeople in my company. I had to

> decide that there would be times when I would do well and there would be times when the other salespeople would do well, and it was really nice for them when they did well and it was nice for me when I did well. What I finally worked through is that selling isn't personal.

> I grew up as a Jewish princess. That's someone who spends her lifetime trying to get her way in one way or another, in a nice way or a nasty way, by wheedling, manipulating, or whatever she thinks life takes. It's something that I've always been aware of because I don't like it in myself. But it's always been there. It's there when I sell because sales is manipulation—you're persuading people to do what you want, to buy what you're selling. Maybe being a Jewish princess isn't as terrible as it's cracked up to be.

Once you get the ball rolling, the ability to sell can be one of your strongest personal assets. Knowing what you are worth on the marketplace and making use of your value is an invigorating experience:

> Once I started selling, my confidence in myself just started building. If I still felt about myself the way I used to, I wouldn't be anything at all right now, because I didn't give anything. Do you know what I'm saying? Let me clarify that. I more or less had an inferiority complex, and it would get in my way because I was so involved in feeling inferior I couldn't give out anything else to anybody. Once I got over this, things started rolling.
>
> Selling is the big thing that got me out of my shyness. I got a job representing a pharmaceuticals manufacturer, where I was forced to deal with the public in situations that were different from any I'd been in. I found out when you're dealing with a lot of total strangers every day, you just can't be timid. The people I worked with were more open than people I'd known before, too. I made friends in business, and everybody would try to

help me, giving little hints on how to talk to people, and how to get what you want, more or less. It's been a great learning experience for me. I still have a lot to learn, because there's a lot more I want to get out and do.

I feel good about myself. I think this past year has made a big difference in my growth. I find myself getting a lot of gratification because I am self-sufficient and dependent only on myself, except for certain emotional needs that are met by my friends and my boyfriend. When I was in school, I never thought I could possibly handle the responsibility of a job and everything that goes along with just growing up. Then I found that once I got out there, not only could I do it, but I was successful at it. Successful in terms of myself, not in terms of business. I mean in terms of self-growth. It's been a very good feeling.

Rewards of Success

The rewards of finding out what it is you want to do in life and then setting out purposefully to accomplish your goal are wonderfully self-satisfying, as Belle, a late-blooming corporate executive has discovered:

There's a vision to keep when you are a kid of what is possible in life, and there's no age you put on it. I'm forty-seven and I bounce out of bed every morning filled with energy. Every morning feels like Columbus discovering America, because once you realize that anything is possible, there are no restrictions on you except those you put on yourself.

Every day is an adventure, which is not to say that every day is joyous. There are plenty of nights when I come home and weep or go to bed at seven because I'm so exhausted. Being in business may not be easy, but it's never dull. Today was incredible. I sold something I've been working on for years, and it's going to be the biggest success of my life. I came home absolutely exhausted with joy. I think I could have made it happen sooner if I'd had mentors and if I'd believed in myself. I wasted ten years fighting the girls-get-married-and-have-children syndrome in my twenties. I hope that girls who are in their twenties now are getting better support as they grow up than women now in their forties got.

Four years ago I knew I was good enough because I had paid my dues. I had been working steadily and it was nice, but I was like a kid with my nose pressed against the glass. You see all these mediocre men who get to be presidents and vice-presidents, and there comes a point when you look around and say, "Hey, how come I'm not operating at that level? What am I doing or not doing?" This project I'm telling you about came at a point when I realized that a lot of mythology had to be thrown out. I had to learn to hard-sell. I had to believe that I was entitled to success because I knew I was as talented as anybody I had ever seen. I had to sit down and figure out what was going on and then work out my strategy. I knew I had to sell differently, to get something different into my tone that people would hear. That's what selling is all about. You have to believe in what you're selling. You don't apologize. You have to know, first, that what you are selling is worthy, and that you are worthy of selling it; then you go to work on the specifics of the selling situation you're in.

Measuring What Success Will Cost You

Measuring the price of your success before you have achieved it is very much like planning goals. What you think you may be giving up may not have to be sacrificed at all, and something you imagined would not change may well turn topsy-turvy overnight. But if you know yourself well, you'll be able to outline what you think success will cost and what its rewards will be.

Think carefully about what success will mean to you and make a balance sheet. Write down what you think its costs and rewards will be to you. Then as you come closer to achieving your goal, look at your list again and reevaluate your feelings about success. Are the costs acceptable? Are the rewards sufficient? Would you willingly do what you've done all over again?

It helps to force yourself to define what's happening in your life and how you really feel about it. And the greatest help may be when the bottom line of your balance sheet reads, "Stop bitching and start winning!"

Reality: *The best feeling in the world is winning at the woman's selling game, and nobody deserves to win more than you.*

Envoi

I believe this is an exciting time in history to be a woman, to be able to declare our independence and our strength, to succeed in whatever way we want to succeed. And this is but the beginning. It is the blossoming of the era of feminine freedom, the dawn of the age when our children and grandchildren become women who can realize their own capabilities, without struggling to overcome the hindrances of a pre-feminist culture. By enriching ourselves today, we enrich the society of tomorrow; further reason to work for and claim the success we desire.

It is my hope that this book will help you in all your efforts.

C.H.